DARK WEATHER

SEQUEL TO FAIR WEATHER

BARBARA GASKELL DENVIL

Cover design by
Grady Earls

For all those who have been waiting to hear the next instalment of Vespasian and Molly's story, the first of many I hope.

CHAPTER ONE

I t woke me. I was alone and as the sleet pelted on the window, I heard the crash of the face smashing against the glass.

I leapt up but the rain was so heavy and dark, it hid almost everything except the thunder. I had seen the huge nose splayed out, the eyes wide open and the forehead a pale jagged stone. Yet now, my own faced pressed against the inside of the window, I couldn't see the face outside and I couldn't see blood, but I could see that the glass hadn't broken.

Before racing outside to discover what on earth had happened, I galloped the stairs down to find Vespasian. He was stretched on the long sofa, reading, with Randle curled on his lap. He smiled at me over the book.

"It seems they have found us at last, my love," he said, his voice soft but lacking all emotion. "I shall have to build a barrier."

I sat down and stared at him. "Who? Burglars? Do we have to build a wall?"

Randle sighed and climbed from his father's lap, settling back down on the cushions while Vespasian stood and reached out one hand. I took it, his long hard fingers closing firm around mine, as he led me outside.

The long terrace, partially roofed, sheltered us from the rain but the drip, drip drummed over the edge of the PVC. But I stood back for another reason. The icy cold and the sluice of damp were uncomfortable but there was also an alien chill and a draught of something strange, seeming far more threatening than any winter storm.

I was clinging to Vespasian's hand and he did not let me go. "I can barricade our home and ourselves. There's no danger, little one," he told me quietly, but the danger I felt was malicious and unmoving. Ice dripped down the back of my neck but this time it wasn't rain. Yet no injured body lay beneath our window and no splatters of blood showed where the crash had occurred.

Looking up at Vespasian, I whispered, "You know what it is, don't you? So tell me."

Still holding me, with his other hand he pointed out beyond the terrace into the soaking darkness of our garden. I saw little except the trees blowing in the rain sodden wind. And then, staring unblinking as though hypnotised, I realised the wind had subsided. There was no wind nor even a breeze to blow at our trees so viciously. Lightning stabbed through the bare branches and reflected in the lake, but something else reflected too, sharp and distinct.

Our garden was haunted.

Unreadable shapes swirled their faded colours. Two – three – more than three. Ghostly wisps stared with black eyes from the treetops and the freeze of penetrating threat. Transparency thickened into solid blackness and the eyes glowed through it.

Narrowed eyes, heavy lidded, gazed back with hungry malice and Vespasian said, "Be gone. Be gone into the darkness. You are not permitted here."

The fleeting shapes shrank, darting back amongst our trees. Yet an ancient voice, bodiless, throatless, cackled like chestnuts breaking under boots. "You are not my master. I go where I choose."

A whisper floated on the wind. "Don't you pity us? Yet it was you who set us free. You might become our master since you destroyed Lilith."

"I am no master of demons nor do I trade in cruelty," Vespasian murmured, "and I cannot pity the inhumans looking to spread misery and pain in a world already suffering."

The shadows clarified. Shapes became arms, fingers reaching, and legs, feet pointing. Faces formed around the eyes but snarled, spitting or snapping. Some, becoming clearer, were coiled serpents, heads darting forwards with eyes red and teeth like fangs.

In the pause, while I watched the horror mounting, turning the beauty of our garden to terror, Vespasian spoke two more indecipherable words and then looked down at me.

"The barrier is complete," Vespasian told me. "I have built what will remain impassable at the edge of the terrace. These creatures cannot harm us. They cannot touch us. But one by one I will destroy any who remain to challenge us."

He led me inside, but I couldn't sit or think of other things. Few now believed in demons and that was a salvation of sorts. But I had been with Vespasian when he had destroyed Lilith. I had even been able to help him. I knew the truth of demons, and I knew what they could become. These pitiful things were separate and although hideous, I knew each solitary thing was, in itself, a thousand times less hideous than Lilith had been. Yet wickedness, malice and venomous hatred in a haunted garden was a nightmare. I felt haunted myself. I walked quickly back to the bedroom to the window where the face had crashed. I dressed in a hurry.

The slam of the rain on the glass panes had diminished. The rain was turning to ice and gradually shimmered into crystal flakes of stunning beauty. It was snowing. The fairy white dither fell from the trees, and the haunting shapes blurred, disappearing into the night.

Vespasian stayed silent and motionless. For some moments our room smelled of dark suspicion and the furniture had disappeared. All I could see was the window, the floating of snow outside, and Vespasian's tall shadowed back.

His voice sounded muted and softly rhythmic as though he was chanting. "Lilith has diminished into the ether for many years to come. But the demons of Samhain come in her place. They wake when she sleeps. She will sleep for a hundred years to come, and hundreds more if I can hold her destruction true for as long as I live."

"I didn't know," I whispered, "and I only knew Lilith was gone. Are you saying these things are like her children? Born of evil? Did you ever tell me any of this? I never understood."

There was a great deal I didn't understand, but Vespasian had not explained. When he appeared so gloriously in my modern world, it was all me explaining to him. Explaining about hot running water and flush toilets, explaining about cars and buses, planes and telephones. Moving from the simplified to the matters I barely understood myself, I had presented the television, music and theatre. Finally, I had presented the computer, something I didn't have a hope of understanding anyway. My new beloved swallowed, tinkered, and began to understand more than I ever did.

He'd said, "Many of the unseen can pass through the ether. Now humanity has caught up, it seems. I find it logical that your telephones and computers can speak through space."

But it was now a modern life, and nearly a thousand years since he had slaughtered Lilith and all her power. I had never known, never been told, of the complications that might remain.

Lilith would eventually return. The dead becoming undead.

Yet in the meantime, the power she had concentrated within her was free to take back its separate shapes and challenge where it wished.

The ice swept our room and the fury remained. The malice sucked at the corners, a ghostly haunting of moving shadows.

I was trembling, unable to stop. The fear ate into me. But Vespasian turned from the window to the darkness where I now sat with Randle, hugging him as tightly as I could, and spreading both arms wide, Vespasian spoke and something sparked. The lights sprang back, and once more, our room was the comfortable space I had decorated just a few months ago.

Randle was still cheerfully absorbed in his book, and I realised that only Vespasian and I had seen the haunting and the black threats. That, at least, was some small consolation.

The snow dither turned from the magical hush to the fierce ice of hail and then, after only moments, back to rain. Even that seemed less than before.

I was searching for my gloves. I told Vespasian, "I need the Post Office." It wasn't worth driving, since this was tucked into a corner of the local chemist, just three minutes down the road at the edge of the village. "I want fresh air too," I added. "And since I can't go out the back, I might as well go out the front."

Forehead puckered, he stared at me. "If they are here, they could also be elsewhere. And it is, as no doubt you have noticed, snowing, hailing and sleeting. At the least, take the car."

Actually, I wanted to suffer anything at all that might banish that other nightmare from my jumbled thoughts, so I told him no, I'd walk. And he nodded, returning to his book and Randle's outstretched arms.

I had always thought the village lanes deliciously beautiful. Ancient cottages cuddled beneath their thatches, windows squeezed into crooked walls and tiny doors squashed between their lintels. Flint brick sank behind the bare knots of wisteria, others nestling behind the ivy. Trees were a fantasy of entwined black arms, curling, crawling and outlining the glimpses of sky between. I breathed out what had horrified me and breathed in what I loved, even though the rain was soaking my hat, scarf, gloves, coat and boots.

Two minutes from the chemist, shaking off the sluice of rain from my shoulders, I saw the next nightmare. Vespasian had said the ghost creatures would be in places other than our garden, but this might have been caused by demon, or man.

The body lay by the side of the lane, partially hidden by bog, by mut, by undergrowth and by puddles. At first, thinking it some poor homeless soul who had collapsed where the shelter of the bushes might help him for the night, I approached the two large feet appearing from the shadows. Well shod and trousers of heavy tweed then denied the possibility of some wretched beggar, and I pushed my head beneath the sedge and thorns.

Calling, "Excuse me. Can I help? Are you hurt?" I thought of a car accident, fumbled for my phone and rang both police and ambulance. Not wanting to wait since the rain made me feel I was walking the swamps, I called out again, "There's an ambulance coming. Someone will be here to help any minute," but then as a last blink of hopeful curiosity, I pushed my head further, bending beneath crooked branches. Immediately I wished I hadn't.

Dead and mutilated, this was the body of a middle-aged man, and what was left of his face seemed vaguely familiar. But I vomited into the slush and stood there, bent over and heaving.

Although shaking and barely breathing, I ran to the chemist and pushed open the door, dripping water on their tiles and gasping. The girl from the Post Office hurried over. I told her what I'd seen, and the chemist came to my shoulder with a dozen questions.

"I don't know," I said in a garbled stutter. "Either a car

accident with a driver that didn't stop. Or murder. It's –
absolutely – horrible. But I phoned for the police and ambulance,
and I think I can hear a siren already."

The ambulance took away the oil-clothed body-shape and the
police, after plodding, searching and talking for an hour, found
us in the chemist's and talked to us for another hour. In the
middle of this, Vespasian phoned, worried that I'd not returned.
He was about to get out the car, but would have to bring Randle
with him since no one else was there to watch him.

I explained. "I'll be back in a few minutes. They've promised
me a lift. No need to come, especially not with Randle."

Vespasian was standing outside the front door under the
porch, waiting for me. The police explained the situation to him,
but had to get away and report back at the station so Vespasian
led me inside, bringing me a towel for my hair while I discarded
every sodden item of clothing by the coat hooks in the corridor.

We went into the kitchen, not willing to discuss such matters
in front of Randle so I put the kettle on and Vespasian made tea.
"Murder? Or accident?"

"Murder," I said. It honestly couldn't have been anything else.

"And who do you know within this area, who would be
susceptible to demonic occupation?"

"Oh shit." I couldn't think. "There's a rude old man who
collects the trolleys for the supermarket but I don't know
anything else about him. There's the postman. He's unpleasant
but again – I don't know him personally. There's the woman who
calls herself a brewster at the cafe in the main square. Do women
do things like that? Do you actually mean one of those shapes
from our garden could be – instigating – such things?"

"Perhaps. Perhaps not. These things travel."

I was slurping the tea, burning my tongue but not caring. I
knew my nightmares would now be doubled. I had started
staring out of the front windows, needing to avoid our back

garden. I seemed to need the natural, unspoiled and tranquil. The pelting sleet had stopped, and the other lane leading away from the village was gleaming beneath the palest sheen of the sun.

Along the laneway, on the side where the late sun now angled, the roadsides were green grass, shimmering with the memory of the rain. But on the other side where the sunshine had not reached, the grass was white with frost. The lane itself was just like a stream, so wet it reflected both sun and shade.

I turned back to Vespasian. "I don't think I can cook anything grand for dinner."

He smiled back. "You make the custard. I'll make the dinner."

We had frozen pizza which they both liked but I didn't, and I made chocolate brownies with custard and Randle jumped up and down and said I was magic.

That was a word I found troubling now and shook my head. "Just human," I said.

"Just Mummy," Randle said.

I plodded over to shove the dirty plates in the dishwasher, and knew I was never going to sleep well again.

CHAPTER TWO

"It's time for bed," I whispered to Randle, trying to control my breathing and my voice.

He nodded and clutched his book, looking down suddenly and kissing the illustration of the fluff covered rabbit on the open page.

"Night-night, Daddy," he said softly. "An' night-night, bunny." He had only recently turned three, but our son's reading ability was improving. But then, as I tucked him up in bed, he added, "I don' like them wotsits, Mummy. I doesn't want them in my cupboard."

I opened his wardrobe door, showing the lack of demon presence.

"Fanks, Mummy," Randle said, curled up and promptly fell asleep.

We had not lived long in this house. It was old but we were recent. Vespasian had bought it for me just six months ago and we'd moved into the huge spacious comfort early in the summer, choosing new furniture as I spread out all my old belongings into this two-storey dream. I even employed a gardener to look after our tiny forest, the huge wooden deck which overlooked it and the vines and twisting avenue of lilac, wisteria and jasmine. The battleground of perfumes would welcome any visitor to the house, leading from kitchen to lake and the little forest beyond.

The village of Wethawand, small, deliciously pretty and very old, nestled in a countryside just as lovely. I'd made a point of getting to know the shop keepers, and the locals I met in the one small cafe. Vespasian walked with me more often than you might have expected, but he made no effort to encourage friendships.

Then the sun bright weather had swung from sweet to vicious and the end of October felt more like the middle of January. All Hallows Eve and the bleak magic of Samhain had increased the freeze and now the snow hung from the bare tree branches like Christmas decorations.

It was too cold to walk on the terrace and too cold to wander beneath the trees, but it was not the winter freeze which bothered me. For the eyes that still watched us were ice too, colder than the snow, and a white so brilliant it had seemed like a fire of silver luminescence.

'They cannot enter our home," Vespasian had told me, and he said it again. Yet I heard whispers in the night and the electricity flickered, blinking out sometimes and pitching me into a blackness beyond the dark of the night.

I went out once to watch the stars when the sky was free of cloud. And there was another reason. I wanted to show Vespasian and the whispering demons and myself too, that I was not intimidated. Yet as I stood, looking up to the sky which was as glorious as I had imagined with its milky spangle of starlight, the moving of the trees without breeze reminded me of my panic. I ran back indoors.

Vespasian looked up from his book. "Call me next time, my love."

So I needed his hand just to go out from my own back door.

I cooked, I cleaned, though without much energy, I read

endlessly since losing myself in someone else's world was the best of all, and I went to bed, making love to my husband. That was when I forgot any fear or any dark moving shadows. Life continued. Yet when I had slept, and then woke, startled, I heard the whispering outside our bedroom window.

"I am the feast that Lilith sucked through her teeth day after day, thriving on each particle of my power which she chewed. Come see my gifts, free now with Lilith's passing. The feast could be yours."

These malicious whispers never woke Vespasian, and I never chose to disturb him. Often, I slipped from the bed and went to Randle's room, but always found him fast asleep and smiling, one thumb sometimes plugged firmly into his mouth.

Then I usually wandered downstairs, but never looked at any uncurtained window. I'd make tea, or coffee, or I'd pour wine, vodka with ice and anything else that seemed handy, listened for moments to the radio, or went to my computer and attempted to write.

Once more climbing into bed, I'd reach for Vespasian's naked warmth, his strength and just the gentle sound of his breathing being my greatest protection.

Twice the police visited, but once it was simply for the courtesy of informing us that a suspect had been arrested, they were fairly sure he was the killer, he was locked up and they would let us know when the trial came up. Probably a year away. The courts were as slow as the great list of waiting criminals permitted.

So it had been the postman who had died, and on Sunday which was his one day off. Poor man. I'd never liked him, but he seemed honest and punctual. Whoever or whatever had killed him, and with no obvious motive, seemed to have relished the act of murder and that meant suspecting the demons.

I didn't investigate.

One afternoon early in December, I sat beside the huge fire in the living room, where the flames danced up the chimney, giant logs piled across the iron grate within the inglenook, I could hear the wind whistling outside but a quietness hung within the room like a heaving mist, settling lower until it surrounded me.

I turned quickly, looking for Vespasian, but could see nothing. Randle was already in bed upstairs, but my husband had been stretched in the chair opposite, hands crossed on his chest and eyes closed, not asleep but thinking. Now I couldn't see him. I knew the mist was between us.

He had been dreaming with the light of the fire, whereas I had been reading beside a table lamp. The five sconces around the walls had also all been alight. And now – suddenly – the lights went out.

My table lamp flickered, popped and died. The other lights in the room flashed over and over in abrupt sequence, and after some minutes of the explosive contrasts, everything went out. Even the fire. The wind whistled down the chimney, and I could hear it whine amongst the ashes.

The flames had gone and the mist closed around me. It was a promise of death. Nothingness.

I sat paralysed, hanging onto the arms of my chair. Again – the whispering. "Sleep, sleep, and sleep for evermore," whispered the mist.

Then I saw the eyes in the mist, raging scarlet eyes with lids of slime. The eyes dripped, drip, drip, and the slime ran in thick trickles of stench across my toes. I could feel the icy dribble. The mist was clammy. I felt myself drowning. The only thing I could breathe was the thickening mist and the crawling stench. I expected to fall, and then hit the bottom. But the end never came.

At last the paralysis fell away and I leapt from my chair like some wild thing, screaming for Vespasian.

Then I was in his arms and the lights blazed and the fire flamed in huge golden waves up the chimney. My book was upside down on the floor, and I had collapsed against the solid reassurance of those glorious arms, muscle, bone, and as hot as the fire.

I told him haltingly, almost stammering, what I had seen and heard. He had experienced none of it. Not one blink of it.

He kissed my eyes and my eyelids, the tip of my nose, and my mouth, hard and hot. Then he tickled my ear as he said what I'd hoped he would. "This is wrong, my beloved, and I shall not allow it. These creatures cannot enter here, but they are gathering enough strength to overpower the electricity, and even, perhaps, your mind."

"What I saw didn't happen?"

"If you saw it, my beloved, it happened to you. The ether carries many things, including visions for the chosen individual. The soldiers born from the sources of evil have the powers you only know from your telephones and your computers. You receive an email, but I will not see it if it is addressed only to you."

I understood. "Am I so weak? Am I so vulnerable? But you said we weren't in danger."

"I cannot be sure," he told me, his fingers through my hair. "So I will fight further, and eliminate what I had supposed unimportant."

How the hell can you think demons unimportant? I stuttered, "I think there's more than there used to be."

"Very soon," said Vespasian, "there will be none."

This was a man who travelled time and who, unbelievably, had learned to love me. When I thought I had seen him slaughtered in medieval England, I returned to my own self and time, now once again without power.

Then he had followed me through the gateway, appearing through the ancient yew tree in the forest near where I used to live, and knowing me as clearly as if I was still his wife. I was already pregnant, and carrying his child.

Randle was born just over three years ago. When new born, I thought him the small round image of his father. Then, as he grew, in many ways he was unusual and in many other ways he was just a gorgeous dark-haired little boy with a delicious smile and bright eyes who learned fast and could already read if the words weren't too challenging. Once he managed transparent but pronounced *trass-pants* and asked if he might have some. He invariably slept well and dreamed deep, then enjoyed recounting his dreams in the morning, telling their stories as if such events had genuinely occurred that night.

I had started labour two weeks before expected, and Vespasian had first telephoned the hospital, and then proceeded to hold me and finally deliver our son just as the ambulance turned up. My pains had been severe but so fast, I had no time to do more than grunt as I pushed Randle into the world. Vespasian put the tiny warm bundle into my arms, kissed both our sweaty foreheads, and went to open the door.

Now nestled in the room next to ours, Randle slept with concentrated determination. We used an intercom, but he rarely disturbed us. When Randle began to run as fast as I could, we had decided to buy a larger house. My Cotswold cottage had been minute. Now just a quarter of a mile from our ancient village of Wethawand in Wiltshire, the house was large, the garden was huge, and the demons had found us.

I blinked through those fleeting moments when I wished we had stayed in Gloucestershire. But I suppose any demonic creature would eventually find its intended goal. They had been playing ever since Lilith's destruction, and needed no more practise.

"Any demon is dangerous," Vespasian had told me eventually, "but I have the power to protect us all. I cannot protect beyond my walls. They can kill, and they can inhabit any soul already dreaming of evil. The police suspect could have been inhabited by some demonic presence, or the demon itself could have murdered any man inclined towards such inhabitation."

Christmas was looming. Vespasian trudged out to the great spruce, thick green, standing at the side of the lake's banks, and took Randle with him. He suggested I come as well and I refused, quite gently as if it hardly mattered, but said I was going to make custard. So they went without me. I knew Vespasian was proving the innocence, the lack of danger and the strength of his own ability to protect us all, but I watched from the window. They hung the tree with fairy lights until it shimmered in silver and every spangle the branches accepted. Randle ran back indoors with a smile that lit his face pink, not silver, and told me, "Mummy, 'tis evermost bootiful. And not one of them tree shape things could come near. Daddy told 'em piss off."

"And they did," Vespasian smiled. "But I have spoken with some, and I understand just how we'll eliminate them. After Christmas, and once you decide your own place in this, they'll be gone. Not entirely easy perhaps, but neither risk nor the possibility of failure will arise." He looked at me. "So will you come?"

He hadn't explained, although it seemed that he thought I should understand. But if he was going, I would too.

"Yes, I'll come. I don't need to take ages over that sort of decision. But who can look after Randle?"

"Time," Vespasian said. "We will leave as he sleeps and will return just one moment later. He'll neither know we've gone, nor see our return."

That frightened me a little. But I said, "Alright. After Christmas. The New Year, perhaps."

. . .

"How apt," he smiled. "Although when I lived before, the New Year came in March. But, my beloved, we shall leave at midnight of December the thirty-first."

"And how long is a moment? Randle can't ever be alone," I insisted.

"A moment is whatever I wish it to be," Vespasian answered. "We will therefore return before one single minute has passed on January the first. And there will be a garden so safe, we will hardly recognise the placid emptiness."

"We can fix everything so quickly?" I knew he didn't mean everything might be solved in five minutes, but I wanted to know more.

With a finger tracing the tuck at the side of my mouth, he said, "It may take a year. It may take two years. But I can take your hand and skip the months between, and we will still return almost at the moment of leaving."

Yet even as we discussed our plans, laughing sometimes, and playing with Randle, other threats swooped into our home.

The Christmas season was not quite over when the long wail of arrival spiralled down our chimney, and when Vespasian strode out onto the wooden decked terrace, I could hear him speaking for long minutes. When he came back into our living room, kicked off his shoes and swung his legs up onto the long-curved sofa, he spoke almost apologetically, "Now there are fourteen. Many have cannibalised others, so making their own power multiply. There is not one which could prove itself stronger than myself. But if, unlikely though it might be, these things bonded and came together, their power would outweigh my own."

CHAPTER THREE

"They feed off each other. Sucking and swallowing, the one a little stronger will absorb the weaker and become stronger still. Over the stretch of years, one may absorb ten others, and feel himself master. But another, stronger still, will pounce, and the first will be sucked into the being of yet another. No demon claims friends, but those already taken within will sit placid, knowing they will spell part of a mightier force."

"We have fourteen. Of what?"

"Call them demons, devils, creatures of the dark, Lilith's orgy, hellion, or any other of a hundred words. Our presence attracts them. Fourteen of the strongest now reside here, watching each other with suspicion, but watching us with greed. And I know exactly how to eliminate such sewerage."

Scrambling from my cocoon, I stood beside Vespasian at the window. There I stared down at the small lake with its lilies and glorious surrounding maples, now bare, and the willow weeping its loss of leaves at the far end. Beyond that, beyond the bridge and beyond sight in many places, but still within our gates, was a small forest that lined our old and broken stone walls. The largest tree was an oak, but the only leaves were attached to the evergreens, cypress and others, including the silver decorated spruce.

Across the reflections in the water, cross-legged beneath the oak's enormous bare branches, sat a little old man, head up, staring back at us. He was certainly visible, but he neither was a shadow nor cast one.

I said nothing. Vespasian had opened the window, his arms crossed on the sill. The rimed panes began to crack their ice as the warmth inside hit the freeze outside. Vespasian said softly, "Triumph, my visitor? You have negated your companions?"

The old man clambered upright and straightened his back. His voice was bell-like and didn't fit his wrinkled face and straggles of white hair from his brow, ears and chin. "Indeed, I triumphed," the thing said, almost singing. "I am the master of my legion and hold the power of the first ten, which has always been my own within the mighty Being of Lilith, and now the power of Fastoon, now within me, and the power of Laquia, now utterly absorbed, I am thrice endowed."

I was peeping over Vespasian's shoulder. "You ate them?" I asked, fascinated.

"I drank them," the thing replied. "I sucked them dry. Others will fly here for the essence of your own master attracts them. I shall wait and absorb more when they come."

Smiling, Vespasian spoke, "You are Inbore, the irritation that brings pain with the broken bone and the cough. You are an insect and no demon. Even containing the others, you cannot rise further than a barnacle."

Although he stood at some distance, I could see the thing's fury for it darkened and seemed less human. Within its outline I could even see the moving shapes he had absorbed. His hands were red and mis-formed into the shape of acorns, tight little fingers like scales over the knot, and the nails wooden. It opened its mouth and showed vampire teeth, both bloodstained. The drips of blood slipped down the elongated chin and clung to the wisps of white beard.

"The blood," Vespasian told me casually as though discussing the winter weather, "is a false impression, since all demons are bloodless, and it has eaten nothing else except their capacity for cruelty."

"I'm going downstairs," I said. "I need a very strong coffee." I was huddled in my dressing gown, hands deep in warm pockets.

Following, Vespasian opened the bedroom door for me and both of us strode again into the living room. I checked on Randle first, then went to make the coffee. When I came back with the steaming cups and quickly looked out of the window, the thing appeared to have gone. I sipped at my coffee. Vespasian swallowed his in one gulp. In his medieval lifetime there had been no such thing as coffee. Now he enjoyed it, and tea, even hot chocolate if not too sweet.

It was over his empty cup that he told me, "That thing is not one of the fourteen. It will quickly be sucked dry. So one of those already stronger, will soon become stronger still." Suddenly I could smell burning, but before I could jump up to check, he caught my hand. "The stink of other worlds, my love. One has trapped the other as I predicted. We once again have fourteen."

The disgusting stink of it faded but beyond the living room window I could still see the waving shadows and the freeze of malign darkness. Above our house the starlit spangle of a myriad stars still promised beauty, but where our garden should have been was now a plague of evil. I felt sick.

He knew, smiled and lifted my fingers, kissing my hand as once a lord kissed his lady. I sniffed. "How long before we get rid of them all?"

"Just a few days, little one. I must still know the past actions of these creatures. What they absorbed and where they lived. I intend to travel back to some past time when at least three of these can be destroyed, bringing the cluster from fourteen to eleven. And if I destroy each before their entire strength is complete, they will be quick and easy to kill."

"You can destroy them before they get this terrifying?"

He was still holding my fingers. "Now come to bed, my little one. We will not dream of demons nor permit them to take over our lives."

"I can't –" I mumbled. "Not with the clock ticking and my heart beating even louder. For pity's sake, darling – how can you think of anything else?"

"Like this," he whispered, smiling.

Back up the dark stairs, footsteps silent on the thick carpet, tip toeing past Randle's room, then into our own. Vespasian shut our door, and lay on the bed, hands clasped behind his head, one knee bent, and smiled at me silently as I hurried into the attached bathroom. I did not lock the door, we never bothered to do that, but I had closed it. It opened while I was busy cleaning my teeth. Vespasian was naked, I was aware of him only as his arms seemed to surround me and his smile appeared over my shoulder in the mirror. He turned me around and kissed me, my toothpaste against his tongue. He laughed and continued kissing, then pressed me hard back against the tiles and started very slowly to remove my dressing gown.

As each button surrendered, I felt his long fingers sliding against my skin, warming me, probing and pressing. His eyes were half closed and his breathing was hard and hot in my hair. When I was as naked as him and twice as aroused, he tossed me into his arms and carried me back to bed.

All I wore was the toothpaste. He kissed it from my lips and his mouth then slipped down to my breasts, his hands to my back and then to my buttocks, pressing hard, whispering in my ear. His breath tickled, but the words were so tantalising I stopped breathing. He told me what he'd do and told me in such stunning crude and decisive detail that I gasped. Then what he'd said was what he did.

An hour later we lay naked together, my head against his nipples, exhausted and utterly at peace. A transparent roof of sublime pleasure seemed to protect us. I couldn't think properly. Murmuring to my ear, his voice was a delicious tickle and the things he said were like the custard on the pudding. The wooden bedposts were heavily carved, but we rarely closed the curtains, cream silk richly embroidered, which rustled in summer when the window was pushed open. Nothing rustled now and the malice outside was gone from my mind.

His voice, always so quiet, was now a whisper. "Each woman has her own curves, each unique and each so precious. Your breasts curve outwards below the nipples, and above the nipples they curve upwards. Yet both curves swell so lovingly, tantalising, each as beautiful as the other." Still in a trance of delight, I heard him like a distant waterfall.

"Such sweet words."

"And when I feel your body rise, I wait to feel the first tremble of your coming. Through my fingers, I feel you explode. And then your explosions echo, with a ripple of pleasure continuing like the aftershocks after the volcano blows. Your climax repeats over and over, eight times perhaps, or more if I can touch where I want." I shivered, the delight rising again. Still naked, lying calm and warm beneath me, he traced down the inside of my thighs. "Must I let you sleep now, my beloved? Then tomorrow shall be another day."

No dreams interrupted my sleep that night, and I woke late to a mild glow of winter sunshine and Vespasian's kiss on my forehead. I yawned and noticed the rise of steam from my cup on the large bedside table, morning tea, and not something Vespasian supplied often.

When I finally staggered downstairs, Vespasian was stretched, long legs in worn out jeans, on the huge armchair in the living room. His own teacup nearby was empty, and Randle was curled on his lap. Still in his pyjamas, he was looking with considerable fascination at a colourfully illustrated book of nursery rhymes. Vespasian was turning the pages for him, but looked up as I rolled in, hair askew and eyelashes still half stuck together.

Randle smiled. "Good morning, Mummy."

"Good morning, darling," I said, still gruff from sleep.

Then Randle said, "There's a lady outside, Mummy. She's not very nice."

I nearly cried. The night had swept my fears away and now they hurtled back into my stomach. Gulping back tears and vomit, I mumbled, "Shit," and leaned over to kiss both Randle and Vespasian's foreheads, my own good morning. But as usual it wasn't a good morning. Looking at my three-year-old son who saw demons, I asked carefully, "Do these things ever give you nightmares?"

He shook his head and pointed to the book he held. "No, Mummy. You showed my cupboard all nice empty. I dreams nice fings. Look, there's a cat wiv a vile–inn. I had a dream about cats and bunnies and foxes. I seen a fox once. Before the nasty pink lady."

I doubted if any wild animal would come into our garden now that it was inhabited by other creatures, but the birds still sang and the late sunrise was still heralded by the melodies and multi-toned chirruping of the birds singing to the pale golden sky.

So a haunted garden could still be beautiful sometimes.

CHAPTER FOUR

The police visited again. I invited them in and just hoped they weren't the sort to see demons.

DI Lawrence told me that the suspect had been on suicide watch yet had still managed to kill himself. I couldn't help seeing the victim's corpse in my mind again. Frost bound hair and lashes, a thin scraggy body stuck in mud, but the face utterly smashed down the centre and one side. One eye hung loose as though on a string. The nose was bashed in and lay splayed whilst the forehead had been caved so that both left and right stuck outwards like protuberant stones, although the middle was a canyon. Both lips were cut, teeth smashed in, and the chin a bloody mess of fleshless bone.

And then quite suddenly I thought of something.

But the DI was talking. "Mr Jones. Derek Jones. No doubt you knew him as your postman, Mrs Fairweather. He'd worked here for years and lived beside the old church. Widowed with no children, and not much liked in the village. He kept to himself. But he had no criminal record nor any reason to be targeted as far as we could tell."

"It's – horrible," I said, feeling sick again, and swallowed hard.

"You would have been required at the trial of course," the police sergeant added. "As the one who found the body."

"But that won't be necessary now," the DI told me. "Our suspect was a young man with a long record of theft and armed attacks, although he'd never killed before. But his DNA was found on the body. Hair and blood left on the dead man's clothes. An open and shut case. The suspect admitted having recently felt ill with a desire to see what it would be like to kill. A feeling of power, he said. Claimed he'd actually found the strength to pick up the victim and throw him against a wall. Absurd, naturally, but there was no doubt he'd committed the killing. Because of his attitude, he was on suicide watch in prison but he still managed to tie sheets together, and hang himself from the fire alarm, kicking the chair away. He was found this morning. So we've closed the case apart from the paperwork. I dare say you'll be relieved, Mrs Fairweather."

I was, having no desire to be a witness at a murder trial. More importantly, the police had now confirmed what I had suspected just moments before. That the wretched postman had actually been the one smashing against my bedroom window some time previously. It was a sickening thought for I also knew it meant demons. No young man could bodily pick up another man, however scrawny, and toss him up to smash against an upstairs window. Yes, the poor sod had done it, but the demon within had been both the inspiration and the strength.

I could understand also why the culprit had hung himself for knowing the sickness of the demon inside, only someone thoroughly evil would remain comfortable.

I attended both funerals. Odd, perhaps. Vespasian, who did not believe in the modern funereal fashion, preferred not to come and that was fine by me. I felt a somehow obliged to watch the sad little cremation of the poor postman since I was, in a strange way, involved. The funeral of the suicidal culprit, convinced that he had been forced into action by one off our demons, seemed just as pitiful so I went to that too, and since the boy had no family, I was almost the only person there apart from the police.

With Christmas over, I counted the days. December the twenty seventh, the twenty eighth.

Then I asked, "Will it be an adventure? Or a nightmare?"

"Simply hard work," Vespasian told me, "but with you at my side, little one, there will be moments when work turns to adventure and you chose to come with me, so that already seals the delight."

I hugged him, and sitting next to him, I leaned my head on his shoulder. "We kill three demons at a stage before they are too strong. And so – not strong enough to inhabit us?"

"They inhabit humans, only when that human already feeds the cruelty inside his own imagination and desires. We are not food for demons, my love, and would not fit on their platters. They can only go where the heart is open for them."

And of course, that meant we'd be going to some time when vile and brutal souls would house the demons we meant to kill. I thought of the billion times throughout history when the world cherished cruelty.

"Wars and battles? Will we risk our lives?"

I expected him to say no, and thank goodness he did. I'd risked my life many times as Tilda and even more often as the Gate-Keeper. But now there was Randle.

Vespasian said, "If we died in the past, as we do in each incarnation, we would still be reborn and be alive here, as we are. Or how would Randle be born? The same isn't true of the demons since they never die a natural death but can be destroyed. Destruction eliminates the future. I have found a time in the past when three of our leaf-leeches are alive and chewing within separate humans. Two more days, my love, and we leave."

He played with my fingers, rubbing my fingertips and squeezing my palm. Finally, he looked into my eyes. "At the heart of all evil is the open road to cruelty. Humanity owns the pathway to love. Whether each soul keeps that pathway open is up to his growth through reincarnation. He or she may turn to cruelty through fear, which is tending towards evil. But the absolute desire for cruelty as pleasure is the demon. Every fragment of evil nurtures this through some unlocked passage. Entering a human soul is the demon's aim, for then he lives."

Each day brought a more horrifying sense of doom. Vespasian's strength which he called alchemy and I called magic, was never going to permit the influence of some petty devil creature into his being. I wasn't so sure about myself. I thought it possible, and once thought my temper was a problem. I had certainly wanted to kill Bertie on occasion but never seriously meant it. My first husband had been my own mistake anyway. I'd thought him a sheep in wolf's clothing but soon discovered that he was the genuine wolf.

I didn't want to ask more questions, so I just muttered, "I promise never to eat one and turn into a serial killer."

He wasn't smiling even though now I was. "Cruelty can be a needle prick, my beloved. The insertion of doubt into someone practicing courage. The expectation of revenge, and even the contemplation of ridiculing the one who has made you cry. But no demon inspires such petty emotions. They bring a far greater cruelty, which, little one, you cannot ever absorb."

Yet I was never sure how much of the nightmare I saw was real, or simply my own fear reborn. I had never before thought of myself as a coward, yet the sense of daily dread leaked into me from that whispering garden. Shadows formed when there was no light to build them and moved when there was no wind to cause it. I smelled the decay of my own courage.

As my greatest protector, my husband was my source of

comfort and courage now, but I felt I should foster my own, and said, "I suppose it seems so grossly unfair. I know life isn't ever fair to anybody, and I suppose the human idea of being fair is all rubbish anyway. But we buy this glorious house, my absolute dream, and we have Randle, the biggest dream of all, and it's been so magical here with you both every day. I mean – you don't even go off to the pub or cycling every morning or join the local gym or build a shed and spend hours in it like other men. So it's been heaven for me. Do you ever get bored? I don't, not ever. But now into this dream existence, we get haunted by shitty demons."

"It is," Vespasian said, "a natural consequence. An unfortunate one, perhaps, but inevitable. Lilith's destruction freed the demons which had been her food for centuries, and since she will be gone until far into the future, the present will be open to those now freed from her hunger."

"You," I accused, "don't seem in the least upset." The temporary destruction Vespasian had brought on Lilith had been hard won, and we had almost died ourselves. Vespasian almost did die, yet instead leapt the centuries and came through time to find me. It had been a time of horror and desperation. Indeed, now I was desperate to avoid desperation. The past three years of peace and love had been so blissful and I begged life to stay that way.

"This will take its course," Vespasian smiled. The tucks at the corners of his mouth were suddenly alight. "You take a step and another must follow. We now have the second step, and there will be a third, a fourth and more. But they will be small steps in comparison to Lilith's leap. She was, as you know, the symbolic embodiment of evil. Now, with the symbolism removed, each fragment of fact flies free. Not all will come to us and most will search for other enemies."

"So in time, after you kill three and come home, and there's still eleven vile things in our garden stopping Randle going out to play - and after a bit, more could turn up. Oh, my dearest, will we ever live here peacefully? Should we sell up and leave?"

"Eleven will not out-match me, little one," he told me, kissing my eyes. "I can face eleven without any doubts. You and Randle will never be at risk."

Several times I went out to the long terrace to watch the sunset or the billowing rain clouds, the Christmas tree that Randle loved so much, and the shimmering reflections of a great flock of birds. Yet however glorious something of nature proved, I could not escape the horror of the shadowed menace.

December the twenty ninth. Two days remained before I once again travelled time.

December the thirtieth. Almost there.

A light drizzle sent golden shimmers past the windows, while a blink of sun was oozing out from behind the clouds.

Our house was built around a small courtyard, open to the sky, with sun loungers covered by tarpaulins during winter. As I passed the window which peered into this paved area, I discovered my husband.

He was stretched on a sunbed which he had uncovered, his book flat on his chest, and his eyes closed. He wore the usual faded jeans, no shoes. None of this was amazing, except that it was raining. I doubted Vespasian was asleep, and with only one day in which to plan, I knew he would be deep in thought as his hair slowly soaked into black ooze, and the rain left his few clothes sodden, washed over his face and dripped into his ears. The rain and the cold would not matter to him. What we were about to do was far too essential to allow other petty discomforts any space.

I'd heard an owl call that night and had wondered if our demon made strange night-noises. Now I saw the tip of a wing up under the overlap of tiles on the roof where it jutted over the supporting beams. Safe within our jurisdiction. The light rain, which gradually soaked Vespasian's hair and clothes, was of no importance to him, and I left him where he lay.

I wandered off and started making custard. Randle loved custard.

I was in the kitchen placidly stirring with my wooden spoon when I blinked from the steam and looked away. Then I glimpsed something through the window. It seemed suddenly magical. I stopped stirring.

The drizzle, a gleaming silver curtain as light as a suggestion, seemed to spin downwards from an arc of luminous colour above. Then I realised what I was seeing, turned off the gas, and stared properly through the glass.

A rainbow and from it the last drops of rain spanned the garden, catching the light as they fell. The rainbow was a full archway and the colours were perfect. The glimpse of December sunshine was rare enough, but this was even more delightful.

With a quick glance at the custard, I stepped over to the back door and pushed it open. The cold rushed in as I poked my head around the door jam. But the rainbow was high, and I saw only its descent. So I stepped out onto the wide decked veranda.

Standing there for some minutes, I admired the beauty before turning back to the doorway behind me. When I heard the voice, I was tempted to ignore it. Yet contrary to my own judgement, I turned and listened. I was neither scared nor interested, simply irritated. The rainbow had blazed out with nature's beauty and now this flash of stagnant cruelty dared to spoil it. Just two more days, and I might be killing these things myself.

It was a female voice, "You are not as I imagined you," she said.

Then I saw her. Way out under the oak tree, a shadowed female shape, her darkness accentuated by the rainbow directly above, she appeared like a broken branch, but moved slowly forwards. Finally, she stood on the far side of the lake and gazed at me across the water, yet her shape left no reflection on the ripples at her feet. I spoke with a tremble in my voice, of which I was ashamed and reminded myself that I was not in the least afraid.

"A demon, I suppose. I don't need to know your name. You have no business here. Go away."

"I exist in my own shape because Lilith does not," said the shadow. Her voice was sharp and high. "The human who destroyed the power of Lilith is therefore my friend. I wish to thank him."

"I'm perfectly sure he doesn't need thanking," I told her. "We'd both prefer it if you went away."

Why I chose to be so damned polite to a demon, I wasn't sure. But I suppose knowingly antagonising a demon would have been worse. I had backed away and was now leaning against the open door. "Foolish human," she replied. "I shall wait for the human of consequence."

"I've no intention of calling him," I decided. "I'm fairly sure you want more than saying thanks."

She had come closer. Floating across the lake, where the rainbow lay wondrously clear and bright, almost making a circle with the arch in the sky above, she now stood on the closer bank, only a spread of lawn between us. As she floated, she still looked more like the bare fallen twigs of a small tree, yet I had begun to see the vague characteristics of a face. The nose protruded in a sharp point, a little like the carrot often used on a snowman. Her mouth was lipless and extremely wide, almost cutting her face in two. More clearly defined, her eyes, although close together over the bridge of the long nose, were black and alive.

Her jagged hips swayed. "I am Highsa," the stick thing called. "With the power of Fastoon, and the power of Laquia, now I also contain the power of Inbore. I am now more powerful than your human male and demand his naked soul for my breakfast."

"Not just to say thank you then?" I pointed out. I managed logic. "If you really contained the power you think you do, you could break the forbidden wall that shelters this house, and speak to Vespasian yourself. But you haven't and you can't so your power is feeble."

Those black eyes were now red rimmed, and the red oozed. It seemed like a malicious threat. I was about to walk calmly back into the house when the thing opened that lipless mouth and hissed. "Inbore already held the power of ten, and then absorbed two more. I hold him within and so hold the power of thirteen. You cannot flout my strength for you are vacant of demonic muscle. I could swallow you in seconds."

I shrugged. "You can't suck on human passivity. You can only feed on cruelty. I'm entirely outside your scope. So bugger off."

She sniggered. "Every human contains some element of cruelty and the eager greed of anger. Retribution. Revenge."

My irritation bubbled. "I'm not Hamlet," I yelled at the thing. "I've never" – Had I? – "wanted revenge. Not ever."

"Liar. Liar," crowed the demon. "You want it now. You leak hatred. You shiver with the desire to hurt me. Kill me. Come – little human – come and try."

Actually, this was not true, and I presumed the thing knew it. I hadn't even considered hurting it. I simply wanted it away and gone. So I said, still angry, "It's you lying. I don't want to hurt anyone. I never do."

Then I remembered my battle back in the early medieval when I had met Vespasian. Times of merging personalities, of loving Vespasian both as sweet Tilda, and as myself. Then the discovery of the third power when I became the Warden and opener of the Gates. Cruelty had been a natural reaction to so many aspects of opposition. I remembered murdering the girl who tried to attack me. I remembered slaughtering many with an absolute lack of care or emotion. Probably I was blushing as I remembered. But when taking the body of the Gate-Keeper, I was her. I was never myself.

Now I was looking at the rabid sluice of blood. The thing opened its mouth wide and two vampire teeth surged outwards, gushing the blood as they slapped against the thing's lips. It waved its head as though blind, but searching for the smell. The source of blood, perhaps. Then it roared towards me. I felt its absolute freeze, the freeze of its shadow and the ice of its rage. Flinging out both my arms, I ordered it backwards. Its smell seemed to be its own covering, a dress woven from decay and the stink of vomit.

I had seen it leap, but I felt no touch, nor the drip of blood or breath. The thing had come no closer nor could it mount the raised terrace. It could neither approach me nor break through Vespasian's barrier.

The voice was shrill yet relentless. "I can give you the power to avenge, to protect and to take whatever will increase your pleasure," the thing now screeched at me. "Courage comes with power. You think I speak of sin or wickedness?" The thing attempted a smile, distorting its face. The tips of its teeth poked past its lips. "And think, human, what you would wish to see and do to another human creature which attacked your child. Would you attack in revenge? Think, female. This arm rams out from the figure, while your child lies at the feet of the same. It rushes forwards. So you rush forwards."

"Rubbish. You speak gibberish."

"You have a knife. It is a steel blade used for decapitating small creatures such as dogs and cats. You brandish this. You ram it hard into this human's bulging chest. But he tries to hurt your son. You cut his skin with the knife. It peels off and you see the bleeding flesh beneath. It is raw. Uncooked. You point the knife into this human's eyes. You blind him, first one eye and then the other. The blood is richly red. And so you are happy. I can give you that power."

Staring back, I grunted, half sick but almost laughing. I swallowed hard and said, "You describe nonsense. And I'd never do anything like that. If anyone tried to hurt my son, I would phone the police."

The spindly elongation which was a leg shadow I presumed, advanced, bending upwards. But the thing could not raise its foot to the veranda. Thrown backwards, it squawked and the black tunnel eyes began to bleed. It spurted blood from its mouth. The blood from the eyes rolled down to the mouth and joined the scarlet rivulets. "The police persons do not come. You are afraid for the little human's life. You wish to kill the big human. The big point of your blade enters the nose and cuts deep. The human screams but you wish to hurt him more and more."

I walked forwards, standing only a foot or two from the thing. Its stench made me sick, but I felt no scrap of fear now and wondered if this ridiculous conversation might help me understand, even help me when I travelled with Vespasian, and would face these things again. Then she lunged at me and her shadow seemed to thrash against me.

Her leap was startling, and I stumbled backwards. Solid warmth caught me.

The thing halted. It now seemed paralysed, mouth gaping, hands lifted with claws curled. The blood dripped from its teeth and fingers and continued to dribble while no other part of the thing moved. It had not mounted the terrace.

"A pointless mock attack," said Vespasian, his voice so soft I could barely hear him. But the thing did. It trembled and crouched down, tucking its hands behind its shadow and snapping its gums shut.

Now the thing was snivelling. I turned, collapsing into

Vespasian's arms. "I didn't walk through your barrier," I assured him. "But when it jumped at me, I was so startled, I couldn't think."

Vespasian set me back against the wall, and walked away. I was freezing again and wished he'd just take me indoors. But I wouldn't run away now, and needed to stay and see what happened. He approached the demon which stood still, watching with squinting distain.

"You cannot hurt me," the thing said. "I am so strong I might crush a mountain."

"A useful talent," Vespasian murmured, "but one you do not have." He walked to the edge of the slightly raised decking and looked down the two little steps at the shadowed thing. Then he reached out one hand and crossed the barrier which divided the safety of our home from the danger of the garden. His fingers closed tight around the narrow twist of shadow which separated head from body.

The thing screamed and struggled.

I heard a snap.

"With the power of all that is holy," Vespasian stated, now speaking loudly, "I command the utter destruction of the thirteen demons here within. Fastoon, come out. Laquia, come out. Inbore, come out. And Highessa, release the demons within, and as you remain utterly empty, surrender to your destruction." He had not released the thing as the other shadows swirled from the staggering shape. Vespasian forced his hand down to the grass, and the thing toppled, its darkness shrinking.

A squealing wail echoed from where the thing had been, some last leaking hatred. "You protect your home but not from The One nor The Other. Two there are – coming – coming – now here and can enter where they wish – here both here – "

Then it was ant-sized, simply a grain of scuttling silence.

And because it was this thing's destruction that absorbed me, and Vespasian's actions that I wished to remember and perhaps copy, I took no notice of the thing's words. It had wailed of furious nonsense, and I only cared for the end. Nor did Vespasian mention afterwards anything concerning the dying demon's obscure threats. He was more involved even than I was, in the immediate destruction.

With the tiny grain of coloured grit, now thrown to the ground, Vespasian smiled and stood on it. I heard a hoarse release of breath and the squashed darkness lay still and tiny, as thin as a blade of grass. Picking this up between fingers and thumb, Vespasian blew on it, hot breath steaming in the cold. That minute grain disappeared.

The other released demons seemed drunk, falling, wobbling and crying out without words. Vespasian called each of them to him, and they seemed quite unable to disobey. As they came, so he strangled them in silence. Flailing then disintegrating, they shrank as the first had. Vespasian seemed to blow downwards, his breath like an exhalation of mist. Then each was crushed beneath Vespasian's bare feet. He continued to blow until I saw that his breath was curled like squeezing fingers.

I said, "You should have worn shoes. You have bits of demon stuck to your heels."

He laughed and lifted his feet, showing clean and unmarked soles. "A destroyed demon disappears, since it is a deed undone, and has no body. It appears, but is illusion."

"Symbolic again?" I asked.

"No. the symbolism died with Lilith. It will be many years before she can rearrange her symbolic magnetism."

"Then?"

"These putrid things are the instigation of intentions." He took my hand again, and the reassurance of his touch was immense. Now I absolutely knew safety. "Until the act is done," he continued, "these demons have no substance. You refused their control, their temptation and their open messages. That denial, my little one, has left them weaponless."

In the house again, the warmth was a caress, and I could smell custard. Randle was still asleep on the sofa.

"Are they all so – pitiful?" I asked hopefully.

"Cruelty is always pitiful," he murmured while pouring me a glass of Baileys. "Kindness is strength and so it can be hard to maintain resolution. Cruelty is the pitiful reaction of fear and stupidity. But," and he handed me the glass, "now we have only thirteen creatures haunting us. Tomorrow night we will begin the voyage ending with the annihilation of three more. Then there will be ten. And each as easy to kill as this was." He smiled, adding, "as long as they remain unattached. If they manage to band together, then I must still prove invincible. But it will be hard work and take some time and effort. If I fail, well, the failure will somehow need to be overcome."

That seemed suddenly less convincing, but he was kissing the side of my ear while I gulped down the Baileys.

CHAPTER FIVE

The thirty first of December, and apart from the excitement beating holes in my stomach, it was a normal day.

I had already prepared the clothes we needed, indicated by Vespasian as he further explained our mission. As usual for a woman in the past, I would wear neither bra nor knickers.

I always felt uncomfortable without underpants but then I remembered back in my previous home, a little cottage in the Cotswolds, when Vespasian had swum through time, coming to me in the modern world which he would take many months to assimilate. It was only two days later that Vespasian had abruptly turned towards me, hooking his hand up beneath my T-shirt. His fingers slipped easily into the cup of my bra, sliding so softly down to the nipple. He kissed my neck as his fingertips explored my breast.

"This clothing you call *bra*," he said softly, "is so sadly defensive. The other items now fashionable amongst women are a contradictory collection of uncovering, purposefully exposing most parts of the anatomy. Skirts' hems only across the high fulness of the thighs, and legs in black material so tight and so clinging that nothing is hidden and the arse covered only by the colour. Neither frivolous nor unattractive, I find your clothes deliciously alluring. Except for this one item – the bra, as you call it. The breast hiding so timidly beneath, it calls to be discovered."

I still remembered that conversation as the sun created rainbows in his eyes, and his lips rubbed hard against me. I had gulped, and said, "Some women don't bother wearing them,"

"But some women," he murmured, his tongue on my nipple, "do not interest me, my love. A man feels only his groin when he sees his own beloved woman naked, as I have seen you only twice, and dream of seeing you again."

I hadn't told him at that time that I adored seeing him naked too, and thought him beautiful in every way. I remembered once telling Bertie, my first husband, "How can any fool of a man imagine there's any such thing as Freud's ridiculously conceited penis envy? No woman finds a scrotum gorgeous."

And yet now I did.

"But you look," I accused without frowning, "and see the allure of other women, or you wouldn't know our fashions." Personally, I wore neither skin-tight leggings nor skirts up to my arse

But he said, speaking between kisses, "The curve of the buttocks is unpredictable and exceedingly individual. Everything is of interest. But only the woman I love can ever stir the desire between my own legs."

I kissed him back. "But I have to wear a bra," I explained. "Or other men would stare and I don't want that."

And then Vespasian had said, "My beloved, I want to carry you outside and lay you on the grass in the soft morning dew as the stars flicker their last spangles before the dawn. There I shall undress you, piece by piece, with neither bra nor those female braise to hide my view. And then I shall open your erotic privacy, and know each particle of you, and finally take you to me as the sun leaks over the horizon."

At that time my little garden offered no privacy, though when we'd moved here, Vespasian had led me into the mild summer nights to make love in the grass.

Being happy had grown to be a habit. This was the first time that the habit had shaken.

But now I tried to block memories, even those I adored. It was the future I needed to face, so I not only avoided memories, I also avoided windows. Our clothes were laid ready, and I bustled downstairs to make tea, coffee and hot milk for Randle. Vespasian had already dressed our son and carried him to the kitchen. But when he saw me, he pointed to the window. I saw nothing. Randle pointed, dripping the morning custard. "In our nice trees. Look, Mummy," he informed me. "Nasty piggy face. Meany to the trees."

I raised an eyebrow at Vespasian. "Crouching beneath the bare branches of the old oak tree," Vespasian murmured, "are two entwined shadows. They feel no empathy towards each other, but they know that combined demons have greater power than one alone, and are therefore attempting to unite. A complicated process for the essences of cruelty. Before considering the absorption of one over the other, they must fight to discover whether one is already the stronger, while their natural inclination is to terrorise each other."

Very gradually I could make out the twisting of shadows. Randle, disinterested in such nonsense, had returned to his breakfast. "Look, Mummy. I'snear finished all your lovely custids."

"Good boy," I said, distracted, turning to Vespasian. "If one eats the other, we'll be down to nine?"

"Indeed, my love. The fewer the better, which is why we travel tonight. Yet it is easier when they are weaker. Destroying each tiny force of evil would take me an entire incarnation. If they are compliant enough to evolve into compilations, I'll have less to fight."

"One terrifyingly strong demon is preferable to several little ones?"

"As long as none discover a force greater than my own."

And that was impossible since he had vanquished Lilith, although not entirely alone.

Now Vespasian and Randle were both staring out of the window, so I felt drawn to watch, and stood, spoon in one hand and coffee in the other.

The shapes were not equal yet they fought with equal malignancy. Not a fight in the sense of grappling, or wielding a knife. They blurred, limbs mingling, thin coloured wisps of shadow raised and fingers the length of the arms clicked and waved, forming signs and strange elongated signals. One was the taller, a thin twisting blue shadow which bent over the shorter. It was darker, like the oak tree. Their fight seemed almost a dance. Feet like bare branches leapt, then fastened together as they kicked upwards, becoming one branch as they merged with the arms. I was feeling both sick and fascinated. At least in the kitchen I couldn't smell the vile reek I knew would be blowing around them.

"Mummy, 'tis funny," Randle said suddenly, down from the table and now grabbing at my skirt. "Let's open this window."

I said no, but I laughed. Then I felt sick again. The shorter and darker shadow was now drumming its misshapen fingers against its own head, and the round black cranium smashed open. It seemed to gulp, and the thin blue shape, wriggling as though desperate, disappeared inside. The dark head snapped shut. The blue demon was gone.

"And now there are twelve," Vespasian said softly. "And when we return, then there will be nine."

Collecting Randle, he deposited the child back on his chair at the table. I had made his morning porridge with custard, a thick gooey mess which had proved extremely popular. He had nearly wiped the bowl, but a little remained. Randle waved his porridge encrusted spoon, then tapping it with horrible repetition on the table top, he asked, "Will the demon stay outside, Daddy? Should we invite it in for lunch?" Managing to puzzle his father was a rare occurrence, so Randle continued, saying, "Thems done fightin now, yes, Daddy? Ortened we invite the black one wot was winned inside?"

Vespasian regarded his son. "No, little one," he said. "That demon is a fool, and an unpleasant fool at that. We will pretend we haven't seen it.'" Vespasian returned to his third coffee, and Randle returned to his porridge caked spoon.

I took Randle's spoon and wiped the mess from around his small eager mouth. "Good, Mummy," he said. "And I've finished brekky now. Can I go and play? I won't go outside."

"Read a book," Vespasian suggested, nodding.

"I want to play with Tigger and Pooh," Randle objected.

Vespasian had learned to drive in only a few days. Television surprisingly bored him but he loved to drive, enjoying the versatility of vision from a speeding vehicle, and now we owned two cars.

Money seemed to fly from the heavens and I questioned this only once as I gazed at our two luxury cars sitting smug and clean in our equally spacious garage. He had raised an eyebrow. "You question an alchemist regarding his gold, my love?"

So – memories again. Pointless memories. I knew the overwhelming itch of excitement yet at the same moment, facing the future reminded me of the danger.

Vespasian bent over me, kissing the top of my head. "I'm taking Randle out for a short drive into the village," he told me now. "I intend on buying us both torches, tiny enough to be hidden in our clothes but still bring light to a world without electricity. It will not take me long. Will you come?"

I had an idea which suddenly seemed important to me, so I shook my head.

"Not now, my love," I said. "But please don't be long. I'm making a pie for dinner."

One eyebrow raised. "Rhubarb pie and custard?"

I laughed. "Steak pie in red wine." And I watched him march out to the garage with Randle, smothered in warm coat, scarf, gloves and woolly hat, ran after him. Vespasian never seemed to feel the cold. Now he pulled on an unlined jacket and seemed to think it enough, even though he had prepared Randle for the greatest snowstorm that ever blew. The engine started, and the car reversed into the lane. I stopped watching, left the oven on so that I had to remember the time and limit my idiot intentions, and crossed to the back door.

Across the misted banks of the lake, the forest merged into glimmering hints of colour. Although the sun was unseen behind the darkening clouds, a blur of russet wavered as though it might have carried shape, but then had lost it. The oak tree, branches bare, blew in a wind which did not exist, and a birch, its slim trunk usually white smudged with black, now seemed to contain the flowing red shape of a woman within, her hands emerging from the bark, then disappearing. The entire tree bent, then straightened, then bent again. The birch tree was dancing although no music accompanied her, and the oak moved aside.

I stared, disgusted. The demons even though now fewer, were stronger and had taken over my garden. I could not count what seemed so elusive, but I could smell anger, and it wasn't my own. Even the tall sycamore now seemed cruelly alive, its branches twisted and leaves scrunched as though squeezed by hands.

The destruction of these monsters was surely beyond me, but I had watched Vespasian and I remembered every action.

Yet the one thing I still feared to do, and which I believed would be utterly foolish, would be to walk through the invisible barrier and approach those blustering trees, mine though they were, which I had loved so deeply when we chose to buy the property.

They were mine no longer.

So I stood on the terrace with a thick cardigan held tight around me, and stared out. I was turning away when the thing jumped, tiny legs bent like a gnome. Still on the terrace, I gazed back at the thing on the grass not far from me.

It was shaped like a child of perhaps four or five years old and its face was cherubic, hands small and soft, legs and feet in leafy greens. It stretched out pleading fingers and suddenly began to sob.

"Help me." The voice was piteous and weak, just a childish squeak. "Save me." Falling to its little knees, it pleaded, crying again, the tears marking the small round cheeks. "I am lost. I beg to be saved. These creatures will eat me if you don't take pity."

The thing was adorable. But this was no little child abducted by demons.

The pitiful child opened its mouth and vampire teeth sprang outwards, oozing blood. It screamed and swore. The cursing was so vulgar, it made me laugh.

"You don't even know what those words mean," I shouted back. "You're just a demon. You know cruelty, not love."

The dimpled baby screeched, hurling stones at me, but the stones rebounded against the invisible barrier.

A rich blue face peered through the oak leaves. "I wish nothing against you. We are free because you slaughtered Lilith. It will be a hundred years before she can steal us back and imprison us in symbolism. You are my friend, not my enemy. But you must give us our saviour."

"He is almost one of us," screeched a thing in the birch tree.

"So close. When he joins us, he will be the greatest of all. Together we will be the signpost for Hell."

All my determination to practise the destruction of these things, and to increase my courage and confidence, seemed lost. I choked, and ran to the kitchen where I stood panting, as though unable to think. Pouring myself a very strong Vodka and peach juice. Too early, but I didn't care.

It had to be Vespasian, and we both knew it. I welcomed the chance to help, but it wouldn't be me killing these creatures. The plan he was about to enforce would be principally for himself. A man who could see and understand such things would take the arrival of danger as a package addressed to him. A message saying, 'Deal with this as only you can.'

The evening, was now approaching the time of departure. The tune of Old Lang Syne drifted into my head. But I wasn't singing anything now. Randle was in bed and fast asleep, while Vespasian was stretched, as usual, on the long-cushioned couch. The old stereo player was softly lyrical with my old CDs playing the music he loved. As Rachmaninov followed Delius, he looked up from his book.

"Ready, little one? Happy? Happiness compliments readiness."

Sometimes I still didn't entirely understand him. I was cuddled beside him watching the television, but the sound was turned to mute as we listened to the music we both enjoyed far more than any film.

"Yes, both," I replied softly. "Ready. Totally ready. And wonderfully happily excited. But scared too."

His arm crept around my shoulders, and he kissed my cheek. "Questions?"

I'd had enough of questions and cuddled back down with the pleasure of Vespasian's close warmth, the swelling glory of the music, and the silent adventures of Tyrion and the dragons on the screen before us.

My husband's life during the thirteenth century had not included books of any kind except the Bible and the occasional Arabic or Latin scroll. Amongst his greatest delights in the modern world was the discovery of literature, both fiction and non-fiction, alongside the fascination of the internet and computer access. But he still liked his books in tangible and printed editions. I had progressed to a Kindle, but we soon had a house of overflowing book shelves.

And perhaps top of his list of splendid new loves was music. The religious chanting had been quite beautiful in his original lifetime, but repetitious. Some equally repetitious dancing music had also existed. The music more often heard was the crudely erotic songs sung in the taverns after a good few cups of ale. Now the variation and complication of modern music hit Vespasian with delight. He spent days, especially out in the summer sunshine, listening to every musical variety he could discover, even those he immediately disliked, but especially those he loved such as Dvorak, Beethoven and a hundred others. It was a few moments later when he interrupted my memories.

"My beloved. We must now dress in the appropriate clothes, and I shall check on Randle if you wish to make the final touches to the food we'll bring."

I nodded at once and jumped up. The old pendulum clock in the corridor was chiming eleven times. One for each remaining demon. No, that wasn't a good association, and I refused to go anywhere near the windows.

Firstly, I followed him into Randall's room, watching as he bent low over the bed, kissing our little boy's forehead, stroking the hair back behind his ear, and whispering words I could only imagine. I crept away then, and hurried back for the very last jobs waiting to be finished.

Amongst many other suggestions, Vespasian had decided to take an old-fashioned basket of food with us, carefully avoiding anything that would be entirely out of possibility for the era. But where – and when – we were going would include the starving and we didn't want to starve alongside them.

Vespasian helped me dress as these were not the sort of clothes I was used to. Mine were purposefully shabby, but his were grand. Not ermine or purple silk, but the clothes of a respectable man, not wealthy but economically comfortable. I, on the other hand, was just a village woman with more brains than I could demonstrate.

Without zips I found those old clothes hard to put on, but when Vespasian grasped his new britches and jacket, he was already stripped off. And now, once again, it was him that I was watching. I was a dishevelled grump most mornings and just clambered into a warm dressing gown, but this was one of the most important evenings of my life, and I was alert to everything. Including the naked man I loved. Now late at night, the chill drifted through every unheated room, but Vespasian clearly had no problem with chilly weather. Crossing the bedroom to close the curtains, he stayed to watch whatever he had noticed outside. I stayed where I could watch Vespasian himself. Almost as tall as the window, he was slim muscled and sinewy. The obvious strength slipped through his body like liquid. His shoulders were wide, hips narrow, buttocks only slightly curved and a little concave at both sides as though once caught between the anvil and the hammer. I thought him utterly beautiful. His skin was hard and deeply scarred in places, but appeared sun-tanned even in winter. He did enjoy outside lounging, and rarely bothered with a shirt, leading to deep colour. But his body was always a mellow skin-tone, perhaps from his original Italian inheritance. Hair rich black, dark eyes, and only light streaks of body hair. Then quickly turning, he dressed himself and turned into someone quite different. Suddenly he was a gentleman of the 17th century, no wig but a wide, feathered hat, and clothes that echoed his hair colouring.

I was sitting on the bed, our basket of food, torches and other necessities on my lap. He came over and stood directly before me, holding out both arms to me.

"Come here, little one."

I stood and he wrapped me against him, almost crushing my head to his neck. I felt his heartbeat, and mine too, strong and steady. I peeped up at him. I could hear the clock chiming and knew it was already midnight. Only Randle could have stopped us now, and we knew he was deeply sleeping.

"Ready," I said.

"Close your eyes, my love," Vespasian told me so very softly. "Think of nothing and expect nothing. Hold tight and do not move."

I was still studiously following those words when I felt warm air blowing on the back of my neck. My hair was pinned up under a starched cap, and I had been shivering. Now I was warm, but I didn't open my eyes and nor did I move.

Birds were calling. I heard the rich gravely caw of a raven, and then the repeated call of starlings. Vespasian's arms continued to hold me so tightly that I held my breath. It was after some moments more that I heard the soft voice saying, "We are here, my love. Open your eyes."

So I did, to a sinking sun across a tangled horizon and the sparks of flames at a short distance.

CHAPTER SEVEN

T he campfire blazed as the twigs crackled and spat and slowly turned to ashes as the meat gradually roasted dark in the embers.

The perfumes rose higher than the flames. Roast pig, blackened, the skin like black daggers. Vespasian's eyes reflected the fire and the tunnels were now burning red. He appeared almost as a demon himself.

I had turned away, disgusted and horrified as the stolen pig squealed in terror when dragged to the butcher's knife. But I ate the meat. It was delicious, and I was immediately hungry.

It was almost night when, with a private nod in my direction, Vespasian left me and sauntered out of sight, aiming for the tents erected for the leaders and their officers. I was staring up at that endless sky, the stars were silver glimmers between the flying darts of scarlet and the huge flames, their tips dancing high in the cold wind.

We slept in our clothes, cloaks pulled across our bodies like rugs. I was shivering as the fire burned low, but the ashes held some warmth, and although now simply bones, claws and stomach, the smell of the wretched pig floated safely cocooned in the smoke.

I had no idea where we were – except it was England. But I knew when. This was the war that divided England in the 1640s, when a thousand skirmishes culminated in the massacre of the Irish and English peoples, the be-heading of the British King Charles I and the rule of Oliver Cromwell.

It was also the time when witches were called evil, and persecuted. Folk believed in demons, curses, and the small animal kept by a witch to be the fetch of messages between herself and the devil.

When I was young, I believed in none of this, thinking it rubbish. That's the modern opinion. But once I became Tilda, I knew a great deal of that was true. Although not with the childish superstitions of the past, for no fetch existed, and the little black cats that were drowned or burned were cruelly made to suffer for nothing. Most of those hanged as wicked, were as innocent as any cleric, more so than some. Indeed, I doubted if witches existed at all during those bitter times, yet I had come to know the truth of demons.

In a long tunic of blue wool, loosely tied over linen petticoats, I was the slattern I had often felt, the whore who followed any army, hoping for food and perhaps even affection. Vespasian was amongst the rebels and would fight, if necessary, for Cromwell. He needed to get close. He would be doing whatever he felt necessary, whereas I was waiting desperately for his return while camping down with the ragged bunch of followers. There was one woman and her boy that I was to befriend. "Agnes Oats carries the demon in its earlier existence and before it came to nest in our oak tree," Vespasian told me. "And she has a boy with her. Perhaps her son."

As yet, I had not met them. So amongst this crowd of simmering and ragged mass of beggars and camp followers, wives and children of those who fought for the future they hoped would treat them more kindly was the woman I had to befriend. They argued and fought, quarrelled and swore, cold and hungry unless they pushed forwards towards the fire, and grabbed the roast pork before every scrap was finished. The heave and squash unravelled tempers, and the skirmishes of rape and stabbing seemed as though the battlefield also stretched here.

Some guarded the barrows of weapons, and once the fighting began children were sent scurrying with arrows, musket balls and pikes, delivering to those who marched, and needed to be ready.

If the enemy were the first to raise their bows, then the loss of the battle could be decided in those initial moments.

I adjusted quickly to the words I had never heard before, the accents and pronunciation alive back then but now lost in time. Yet the language was an automatic adjustment included in the time flash, although there was not much else that I could call easy. In a way, I didn't want it easy. Travelling back in time with Vespasian was the greatest adventure I could imagine although he was no longer actually close to me, and the adventure buzzed like fireworks in my head. I wanted the challenge. After more than three years of luxurious comfort and the caressing silk of utter love, never boring but often predictable, I finally decided my life needed to simmer again.

But I had not yet begun demon slaying.

The camp followers bundled down, eager to sleep unless they were needed to help treat the wounded, bring in new supplies and carry messages. A woman flopped herself on the muddy grass beside me and gathered her skirts around her. "He starts with a cavalry charge, always does. First one – then the second. Tis a great leader, our brave Oliver."

"I don't know him," I said. "I know nothing of him." I sounded as stupid as I felt.

"You know naught of the leader you follow?" She snorted contempt.

I was in Cromwell's camp of believers and had to play the part. I lifted my chin. "I follow his beliefs. No king has the right to do whatever he likes by right of the Lord God. King Charles is arrogant and thinks himself to be another god."

There was no one wanting to squabble with me as long as I kept a veneer of sweet natured simplicity. Actually, I was content to wander. The scenery was not beautiful, but the skies soared and so did the birds. I saw birds I'd never seen before, and little red squirrels scrambled up the tree trunks, nervous of the noise we made.

It was the next morning, the sky still thickly clouded, when a buzz ran through the crowd. The battle was imminent. The king's forces had been sighted, although they had camped on the opposite side of the ridge. Now Cromwell was calling his troops to wake and prepare. A current of excitement ran through the campsite like the waves on the beach. I heard horses neighing and snorting and the shouts of the men calling them to saddle.

We woke quickly, stretching, jumping up and grasping whatever we had for breaking fast. Nothing was prepared, and nothing was what most folk had.

A boy stumbled past me, and I offered him a stale remnant of my sandwich, buttered and filled with egg and tomato. He didn't say thank you. He just cried, opened his mouth, dribbled tears, sniffed loudly and stuffed the sandwich between his broken teeth, all gone in three huge stuffed bites. Clearly, he'd been starving. I'd offered him food because he'd looked half dead already with legs so skinny the fleshless bones were all that was visible, and his arms were just as thin. He was a stick beneath raggy red curls, and he had hollows instead of cheeks.

Having gulped down the last crumb, he ran off and hurled himself into a fat woman I could see close to the fire. So I followed him and walked over. The woman glowered, saying, "I don't know you, lass. You been talking to my Tom?"

"He was hungry." I nodded, looking from his craggy little face to her double chins. "I had some food I could spare so I gave it to him,"

Wiping his eyes and then his mouth on the back of his hand, the child appeared settled, but the woman still frowned. "You wanna share, lass, then you do it, and I ain't complainin'. But share with the old folks as well as the brats."

Wanting to point out that he was skin and bone while she was all lard, I managed to smile instead. "I'm Molly. I don't know your names."

"Ask the lad," the woman said loudly. "'Tis him you done befriended, I reckon."

The boy had closed his eyes and said nothing. I bit my own lip, not permitting myself to be as rude as I'd have liked. But it was an elderly man sitting next to us who spoke, leaning across me to the woman's stare of disapproval. "So, jealous, is we? You watches yer lad eat, and wants more yerself?"

The boy spoke for the first time. "She's me Aunt Agnes. Was here wiv me pa, wot's fighting fer the right. But has bin injured, me pa, and no doubt will die."

I was sorry and said so. Now knowing the woman was not the boy's mother, I partially but silently forgave Agnes for starving him. "Agnes Oaks? I asked quickly. So I had virtually fallen over the woman housing the demon, and now had to stay close. I expected a question from Agnes as to how I knew her second name, but she seemed uninterested. More interesting was the news churning through our crowd in an excited mumble.

The older man, licking the snot from his leaking nose, threw up both hands and yelled, "Parliament has won again, and our men are coming over to celebrate their victory."

"Is the bastard king dead?" chorused several others.

But it was a woman who stood nearby, hands on hips, and roared, "No, the bugger still lives. But he don't reign no more. And he's no king o' mine."

Agnes lay back, hands behind her head, and smiled at me. "So the bugger'll be chucked into prison for the rest o' his life. Maybe get rid o' the bastard forever and ever. I reckons they'll chop his smug little brain from his skinny neck."

Although the battle had taken place at a considerable distance from the campsite, we heard the noise clear enough, and I felt more squeamish than I'd expected. The clashing, explosion of the flintlock muskets seemed continuous and the firing of the cannon drowned out all others. Yet most of the men seemed to be armed with only those old-fashioned pikes, gathering in circles with the points outwards, a simple defence. What I hated most, cuddled there in the damp mud, were the screams of the dying and the roar of the onslaught. The horses screamed too, as they fell in pain, and lay injured.

Some of the men, summoned from their beds to fight again, were armed with little more than a knife or a sword handed down from Tudor days within the family.

The woman next to me said, "Sometimes they go on all day. Or it might be over in minutes."

"Where are we?" I asked.

"Naseby over the Ridge. Don't you know nothing, girl?"

She was probably younger than I was, but her face was lined and haggard, and her hands were pock-marked.

Agnes was complacent, unmoved by the clash and the screams. I smiled at Tom as he crawled to his aunt's knee. "You've had a hard life?" He stared back in total silence. So I turned back to the woman. "So is his mother dead too?"

"Me nephew? Stupid kid. Thomas."

Again, I looked at the boy. "You stay with your aunt?"

And again, the child refused to answer. I wondered if his aunt actually starved him. Or perhaps he was frequently beaten if he said the wrong thing, so preferred to stay mute. I was guessing, but she seemed somehow unpleasant and knowing of the demon, I thought her capable of a good deal.

The sound of the fighting was fading. The victors were moving. I had no intention of following. The woman was frowning. "Cromwell is bound to win now, I'd say, though the king's men were in greater numbers. But I reckons if he done took the bastard king, there ain't no one left to fight against us no more."

"God's will?" I suggested.

Her frown turned to a scowl. "That's proper common knowledge, lass. We knows the great Lord God to be on our side, for the bastard they calls king be a traitor to heaven. 'Tis our beliefs wot is pure. Reckon t'won't be no more dancing nor singing in this God forsaken land when Master Cromwell takes his rightful place."

It had been misty with a low dripping fog throughout the early hours, but now the June sunshine had oozed through and a pale warmth seemed to please the boy. He sat upright, looking around. There were few easier ways of speaking friendship to strangers than to offer food. This was the time of the Little Ice Age, and food was scarce.

Later that day as we packed out, preparing to move on, I offered Tom a second half sandwich with home baked bread, no butter, but thick fillings of cheese. He shrank back as though I'd offered him poison, then peered hopefully over his shoulder at his aunt.

She nodded and at once he snatched the food, cramming the entire sandwich into his mouth, rescuing each crumb, and chewing slowly.

"But I's mighty hungry too," she said, sticking her snub nose close to mine.

I had more, but I didn't answer since the noise around us was overwhelming. An old man, limping, pushed his way next to me. Two other women, one with a sleeping baby tucked into her shawl, and a younger man, leaning on a crutch, sat closer to huddle into the small patches of unshaded sunshine. It seemed that the sight of food attracted an immediate crowd.

The young man balanced on his crutch and asked me to help him sit. "Or t'will be other leg broke an'all, lass. So give out your hand, if you will."

One leg had been amputated just above the knee, and was still thickly bound in linen with a blue stocking wrapped over the stump. I helped him sit.

"I's Francis," he said, smiling. "Lost me leg at the last fight over in Saddleworth, and it ain't proper healed yet. But I'm living, which ain't true for three of me mates. You gives me some o' that food, lass, and maybe I'll live a mite longer."

He thumped one of my own legs, as though testing whether it was flesh and blood. I pretended not to mind, although I did. "I'm Molly," I told him, "and all in one piece. It must be hard to lose a leg."

The first woman nudged me with her elbow. "Don't encourage the bugger or he'll have you under the bushes by nightfall."

I fiddled inside my basket, not sure I had enough to share, but brought out the bread, the cheese, and the hopeful smile. This time I even managed to give something small to bloody Agnes, and a crust to Tom.

CHAPTER EIGHT

That evening, with the small sun westering and the camp followers gathering once more around the fire, I waited for Vespasian to come back to me. We were a smaller group, most having trudged home with those family members they had been following. But others, too far from home or without a home at all, still shuffled towards hope, and lit the fire that kept them alive.

The flames gusted high against the last fading colours of the sunset, golden points flaring up against a pale lilac and a flat pink line where the horizon sank from view.

I was equally homeless, and equally a follower. But it was Agnes I was following. Tom's father had died, but Tom did not appear moved. There was no special effort given to the information, but a limping woman staggered down with the news, and I assumed she had come from the smaller camp where the injured lay on mats while some received a doctor's help, and others, too close to death to warrant wasted time, were left alone to die.

"You he lad Thomas, son o' Warren Oats?" the woman shouted at one young man sitting near.

He shook his head and pointed to Tom curled next to his aunt.

The woman limped over, clutching her skirts from the mud. "You Tom Oatss?

Well, sorry, lad, but your pa died an hour or so past. Battle injuries, that is, so you can say your pa died a hero." Just an inconvenience, perhaps.

Even I was hungry now. But then two of the boys, cheering and waving their arms, bows slung over their shoulders, hurtled amongst us, pulling the carcass of a young deer they had poached. Quickly the dear was strung up on the skewers above the fire. Its skin crackled. I just felt sorry for the deer, but I also felt sorry for the women, men and children, all of them desperately hungry. Agnes Oats no longer sat close to me, but I could see her boy crying, begging for food. I watched as Agnes slapped his cheek, knocking him backwards.

"We's all hungry. You least, cos you ate wot that tart give you yesterday."

But the child was still skinny as a knife blade and would need a great deal of filling up. Then I thought of tape worms. Abruptly someone tapped me on the shoulder, and I knew Vespasian was back.

The soft voice in my ear murmured, "We will walk. I shall speak, but without being overheard. There is a good deal to say."

No one else was interested since the roasting meat and the baking bread were far more exciting than anything else, so I scrambled up, slipped my arm through his, and walked with him away from the heat of the fire and the noise of the crowd.

Parts of the battle scene lay open, its destruction scattered across the fields and the high ridge, the grass, the mud and the rocky outcrops.

In the mud, some partially obscured by thorn bushes and the leafy scrub, the dead still lay. Their blood had dried and turned black as the roasting fawn, smothering arms, bellies and faces.

One corpse hung twisted within the thorn cradle of a bush. Leaves dripped blood but the once living man now lay without legs, his crotch a jagged mass of wounds and his head almost lost.

I heaved, and clutched at Vespasian. He turned away from the rise where there was no visible sign of the battle recently won and lost the previous day, although I could hear the hoarse chuckles of the victors as they ransacked the dead, taking money, weapons, rings and boots.

Vespasian said, "Eradicating a demon without killing the man it inhabits, is sometimes a challenge, and sometimes easy. But Cromwell, the hero of this battle, holds a crouching shadow inside and his guts are swelling with it. He rages with the misery of his youth and his hatred of the king he considers vile. His fostered desire for revenge is unknown to him. He considers it rightful and needful, and thanks his god for the chance to exercise it. His convictions and puritan values are so vital to him, he believes he should rule the world. And so the demon creeps in and fosters cruelty in the name of holy justice."

"One of our demons?" I asked.

Vespasian's eyes narrowed, but he laughed. "Ours? Perhaps we might call it that. The growing embryo of a creature seen within our grounds amongst the trees. One of the twelve."

"And I've met Agnes Oaks," I told him. "She doesn't seem too bad, although I admit I don't like her. So – can I destroy the demon as you did before?"

"There is one more, perhaps the worst," Vespasian told me. "An unpleasant lord of the land who has fostered the demon of cruelty for many years. And if we destroy these three, that will leave our home safe, for my power exceeds that of any nine remaining. Although to be sure of the destruction, you will help me greatly, little one, but I must enforce the final annihilation."

"So I can't be the final killer." I was relieved although I had wanted to try. "And I can't help with Cromwell. But the others?"

"You, although as yet I am open to circumstances, will be the one who makes it possible for me to destroy the others. You are, as always, invaluable."

I was surprised when he kissed me, since I knew myself filthy and must have smelled horrible. I imagined the collected sweat and the ingrained mud, not to mention the ingrained grease from pork, venison and spills of ale. I doubted I had ever stunk worse, even as Tilda. Vespasian, on the other hand, was his usual elegant and delectable figure. Yet even he couldn't have managed a hot bath over the last few days.

Then Vespasian left, returning to the final cluster of soldiers who had stayed to clean, killing off those still lying near death, and re-routing the barrows of weapons. He would join Cromwell's side as they rode back to London, meanwhile I trudged back to the campsite.

It was easy enough to see Agnes munching on meat wrapped in a wedge of bread, juices slipping over her hands. She licked her fingers. The boy Thomas sat watching at her knee. I dumped myself beside them and looked at the boy. "Was the meat gorgeous? So you're not hungry anymore?"

He started to cry yet again, gulping noisily as he swallowed back the sobs. Agnes glared at me. "He ate earlier. You gave it him, whereas I had naught." The boy shook his head but said nothing. "He eats alright for his age," Agnes said, mouth full.

In a time of hunger and bitter loss, a freeze that killed crops and a war that split the country, I found the woman's greed and the deprivation of the boy more simply selfish than actually cruel. But I edged my way over to the fire, and approached the large man pulling at the remains of the venison carcass. I said, "Neither I nor that poor young boy have eaten yet, sir. Is there enough left for us to have?" I smiled, more piteous than seductive, and the man paused, deciding.

"'Tis the last o' the cheat bread." He handed me a small wedge grubby with baked mud. "And there be gristle here, and wot's left on the bone. There ain't no more."

I took what he gave me and carried it back to Thomas.

He buried nose, teeth, tongue, chin and tears in the parcel, and ate like a piglet. Agnes scowled at me as always. "You give to the boy again. But naught to me."

"You've eaten well already," I pointed out. "And so have I. He hasn't."

Nor had I, but this was of no importance. I wasn't hungry. Vespasian's kiss would feed me for a week.

I lay down to sleep, curled against the bodies around me, human warmth generated, and the boy, lips still sticky with meat juices, laid his hand tentatively on my shoulder. When I woke, he was still grunting. But Vespasian's voice stopped me shutting my eyes yet again.

We walked, and there were no longer corpses and the mangled remains of the dead lying at our feet as we followed the higher ground and then into the shallow valley and the trickles of a stream.

Plodding, back sore and feet in blisters, I passed the hours remembering – scenery – bedtimes with Vespasian – and finally what he had told me earlier.

"The older man is Arthur, Lord Harrington. Avoid him. The demon he carries is already rich in cruelty. The man was already vile. He and the demon attracted each to the other."

"I haven't met him yet."

"You will. What is meant will come to one of us. But I know nothing of him, of his home, his family, or his status."

I had mumbled, "If you see him, remember to point him out to me."

"And in reverse," he'd added, "although I believe recognition will be easy since I'll see the demon within before I see the man."

It was easy to agree to that. "And Cromwell?" I asked him.

He told me.

Cromwell was dark with a permanent expression of dislike for the world of men, but he spoke with charity and care, his pronunciation was of the upper-middle-classes, and he paraded his education.

"While under my command," he told his men, "you'll not steal nor quarrel with your companions, misuse the women you meet, nor kill the livestock in another man's fields. I have supplies enough to keep you well fed, and you'll battle fairly in the Lord God's name."

Vespasian had undoubtedly raised an eyebrow. "I believe the pork roasting now has been stolen from some villager's shed. Otherwise the supplies you provide are insufficient for either army or followers," he told the other man.

"I'll judge," Cromwell snapped, "not you, sir. And you'll not speak again unless I command you." But it was not much later when Cromwell turned, for Vespasian walked close at his side. "I should tell you, Master Fairweather, that it's the troopers who need food, since they fight voluntarily, and need strength to wield the pike and sword."

And immediately Vespasian asked him, "Every army since the Romans ruled Britain, has stolen their food as they trek to the battle sight. But you lead with greater charity. What reason then? Because the Lord God tells you to fight in His name only if you preach the good fight? Or because you need your men to think it?"

Without the smile of recognition, Cromwell had told him, "It's the good church that speaks through me, and I am neither fool nor sinner. The men will steal food whenever they can, and I know it. But I cannot preach it. They must respect me as the Lord's agent."

"And the dead fly off to heaven and are welcomed for their heroism and good deeds?"

Cromwell had raised both hands to the darkening sky. "Naturally. But there are yet many misunderstandings to be ironed in the new church, behaviour to be modified, and I'll not fight for a church which fails to lead in every one of the Lord's commands."

"I had imagined that you fought against the king rather than for the church," Vespasian said.

"It is the same thing," Cromwell had answered.

"Even though the king also believes fervently in the Lord God?"

Cromwell stamped his large armoured foot and snarled. "The wrong God. A virtually Catholic God which cries out for wickedness, singing, dancing, liberal behaviour in the bedchamber, and flattering language from priest and lord with the hypocrisy that follows, being forgiveness only once the coin is passed."

So Vespasian had prompted, "You'd pay no priest? Nor the woman who cooks for him?"

Spluttering as though the thought was a stone in his throat, Cromwell, narrow-eyed, glared at Vespasian. "I thought you a man of knowledge. You should know that coin is sinful, and that every woman must keep to her proper place. She cannot preach, nor can she criticise her husband, nor speak out of turn. I love my wife and daughter, but they know to hold their silence and obey their husband's and their church's commands."

In one blinding thrust, Vespasian watched as the inner demon stared from the man's eyes, the gleam of fire as bright as the campfire flashed between the lashes, and another face twisted, and then sank.

Vespasian's own eyes answered the demon's. The demon slouched back, yet remained in its reflected shadow. Softly, Vespasian said, "You'd build a church where you could pray in silence? I see the virtue of that. But would you applaud misery as you deny happiness, joy and entertainment to all men?"

Sweeping around and as fierce as a fighting man, Cromwell spat, "You'll not question me, my man. Nor ever doubt my knowledge of God's will." and he turned the second time and marched ahead, disappearing into the gloaming.

It was Vespasian who smiled. He now knew which demon inhabited the man, he knew how to destroy it, and he knew when it should be done.

Satisfied, he had told me, he knew exactly what should come next. Vespasian had then strode back along the grassy bank of the stream. A rising sliver of moon floated on the water's surface, and the tiny silver fish leapt within it, snapping at the last midges flying in the dusk. The sudden trill of a blackbird's song faded into cloud. The sound was musical, and Vespasian remembered the absolute magic he had felt when introduced to the music of the great composers he had discovered in the modern world, and the bliss of the electrical systems by which he could easily hear whatever he wished. It was Dvorak's Noonday Witch he had last played before transmuting into the years of the civil war in England, and he still remembered the notes which had so delighted him. Now there was a leader who believed in witches and wanted them destroyed, seeing them in the heart of every woman, and who wished to condemn music, and call it the work of the devil instead of the beauty of God.

Then, absurdly, Cromwell had said, "There are demons around us, which hide within the wicked."

Thinking on this, Vespasian had wandered the hillock back to the campsite where he knew to find me.

Yet something else had occurred as he walked the grassy crest.

Striding over the rise, he had met a woman he knew, although she puzzled him in an instant before he'd understood. She was well dressed, unlike myself, and wore deep red silk and a red velvet cloak lined in soft rabbit fur.

Understanding was a bleak twist of the heartbeat as Vespasian now told me.

"You, my little one," he explained. One thumb beneath my chin, he lifted my face to his and lightly kissed the tip of my nose, then my forehead and finally my mouth, hard and repeated.

I had asked, "Me who? I don't know what you mean."

"My dearest beloved," he said very softly, "it now seems that you are already living here within a past incarnation, and you are, perhaps, a spy for the royalists. I do not know your name. But you are as much Molly as Tilda was. This is a complication I will find difficult, since if either one of you faces some great danger, I will be needed to protect and rescue."

"I don't have a – demon?"

He grinned. "My sweet child, you are as demonic as I dream of you within my arms and the warmth of my bed. And at heart, as angelic as you love to be."

"But," I thought about it for a moment, "it sounds as if both of me are on opposite sides. Does that make sense?"

"You and I," Vespasian had grinned, "are on no side at all. But the incarnation you leave behind you in this life is clearly a supporter of the royalists. I have respect for all humanity, and that includes Cromwell, and his ideals are in some manner both understandable and sympathetic. But his housing of the demon is voluntary, the path inwards opened by hatred, bitter memories and the unwillingness to forgive."

I had pointed across to the camp fire, now spitting as the last bones of the deer tumbled in scraps from their skewer and scattered into the ashes. The fire sank but the vivid sparks rose up to the tree tops.

"That's Agnes Oats. And that's her half-starved nephew, Thomas Oats. Which one houses the demon."

Standing against the background of the fire, it seemed as though Vespasian was as black as the devil, and the scarlet sparks sprang up from his head. "Both," he told me. "Now it inhabits the woman. When the boy kills her in a few years, the demon leaps from her to him. But I shall take the demon before that, and change history. The boy will remain demon free and the woman may live on." The moon was rising and had tipped Vespasian's black hair, spangled in fire-sparks. "But they must wait since the demon nursing on Cromwell's resolutions is the stronger and affects more of those around him." He took my hand again, leading me ready to leave. "When you sleep tonight," Vespasian continued, "think on the woman I saw, who is you long ago, and ready for you to enter. She carries no demon, but she is frightened. You can help her, but more importantly, she can help you. Fill your mind with her as you drift into sleep."

I knew I would and wanted to know her name. But sleeping on the ground did not allow waking with energy. I felt older as my bones ached. "Is she young? Younger than me?" I had asked.

"When I lift you back into my bed," Vespasian replied very softly, "you will forget how old you are yourself."

Now following the slow drag of the injured, and hungry camp followers, I remembered these words, and wondered what I might do if forced to meet myself. I had been safe with Tilda and together we were the same person, never separate unless I returned to my own world. Now I wasn't sure, but I was intrigued.

Vespasian, before we travelled back in time, had laughed, telling me he would find us a cottage to share somewhere outside London, where we could once again share our bed, and discuss whatever was happening. And when it was necessary to wait out many months, or perhaps even a year, he could blink away that time, travelling ahead to whenever we were once more needed. But none of that had yet become the truth and now I slept in the chill with damp grass beneath me, and our cottage felt more distant than ever.

Even halfway to London, the air was smelling of battle and death. I pulled my threadbare cloak tightly over my shoulders and tried to do as Vespasian had asked me, thinking myself into the mind of a woman I had once been, but had not met yet.

I still hadn't found her when I finally fell asleep.

CHAPTER NINE

I am Sarah, Lady Sarah Harrington, but the title is unearned and unwanted. It comes from my husband whom I loathe and fear.

But I am also Molly, wife of Vespasian who is Jasper, once a baron during the reign of King John. But I don't care about the title either, since it's considerably out of date and I'd be laughed at if I used it. Besides, Vespasian didn't use his title during most of his earlier life and laughs at those who believe a title denotes superior blood. He has no birth certificate of course, but has adopted the name of Jasper Fairweather. So I am simply Mrs. Molly Fairweather.

I creep into Sarah's mind when I want to, but it is confusing. Her home is grand, even grander than my own, and they keep hundreds of hunting dogs. Lord Harrington has his own separate bedchamber, for which I am extremely grateful, as he is cruel. Almost demonic. Even his polite good mornings frighten me. There is nowhere I might call comfortable here, but Sarah doesn't care about the house or the dogs, she cares about the frigid cruelty of her husband, and she cares about her country.

When I am tugged into her mind and heart, I am her. I cannot judge her, or tell her about Molly. When I am her, I've never heard of Molly or Vespasian or the future. But Sarah knows a great deal about demons, witches, evil and cruelty, for her husband is cruel and her religion preaches of black magic and accepts that demons and witches are common across the land. Witches are not burned here as they are in other countries, and never have been. They are hanged. But heretics are burned, and that is terrifying.

My Sarah is considered an insignificant part of the nobility of the era, but I live inside her and know her immense courage and determination.

Slim but large breasted, taller than her bent little gnome of a husband, she was the youngest daughter in a family without title but related to those grander. The marriage was arranged, and she had no possibility of complaint. At the church steps, she had begun to cry but her veil kept her tears hidden.

The man raped her on their wedding night. This was not because she refused him, but because he desired the opportunity for brutality, and to prove his power. The force he used would dissuade her from ever refusing him in the future.

Having met his majesty, Charles I, at several court events, Sarah grew fond of the man, and later fonder of his wife and children. She had no children of her own. Once she had been pregnant, but had never told any other soul except her sister who also feared Lord Harrington and so refused to help.

Leaping from the top of the great staircase, Sarah induced a miscarriage. She begged the Lord for forgiveness since this was a sin beyond acceptance, but the thought of a child born of the husband she feared and loathed, was too terrible to allow. A boy child would be beaten until he behaved as his father. A girl would be beaten and treated with unloving disdain. The unutterable misery of any child and herself as the mother, terrified and appalled her.

She knew that dying herself would be an escape she would accept. Surviving seemed a disappointment. The steps were thickly carpeted and perhaps this saved her life, but she broke both legs and dislocated her shoulder, keeping her in bed and away from her husband's clutches for nigh on two months.

Two months of painful peace seemed her salvation. Bed, soft pillows, an eiderdown of goose feathers and a candle flickering beside her. The maid set a brick in the fire, then brought it to warm her bed. The doctor came every week, and sat beside her to talk of the growing rebellions, the disruption of parliament and the terrible discomfort of the king.

When Doctor Small announced that she might leave her bed at last, Sarah was disappointed, but eager to understand what was behind the devastation amongst the court and gentry. Indeed, the civil war had begun.

Lord Harrington had mistresses enough, but was delighted to reclaim his wife. While he contemplated what he might do to her as she crawled from her own bed into his, he also decided that he would join the revolt against the king. His majesty was no friend.

Now it seemed I had two men in my life, and both, in vastly different ways, were extremely dangerous. From the many years of sharing my life with Tilda, I was accustomed to the strange imbalance, and now at least I fully understood what was happening. I had not understood the first time, and Tilda had been so young and so timid at the beginning. Sarah Harrington was not so young and nor was she timid, in spite of the terrible fear she felt for her husband and lord. As she didn't resemble me much, either in looks or in habits, I wondered how much we must change and grow over the many incarnations we experience one by one.

Vespasian, meanwhile, was befriending Cromwell and at first, I saw nothing of him. I somehow missed him even when I was Sarah and had no idea who Vespasian was.

CHAPTER TEN

He slammed open the door of my bedchamber and snarled at me from the doorway. I was still dressing, both my personal maids at my side as I sat in my dressing room before the lead blotched mirror.

I heard the slap of his whip against the door jam. I knew that sound so well, as did his poor horses. We had all felt the pain of the lash against our naked backs.

"Out," rasped my husband, indicating the door.

Both maids ran. I turned from the mirror to face him. He wasn't smiling of course. He never was.

A short man, shorter than myself, his legs were bent and bandy. His mother, an ancient old crone, had told me that the boy's birth had left him badly formed, since the midwife had hauled him out by the legs. "A breech birth," she had cackled, "And no doubt serves him right. Had I known then what manner of person he'd become, I'd have thrown him out to the sewerage."

She was dead now herself, but my vile pig of a husband still lived and offered no sign of caring for me nor for anyone else.

At first, I had tried to sympathise. The short, bent legs must have turned self-pity to hatred of all those better formed than himself. He would have been teased by other children. Perhaps he thought our Lord God had tortured him without reason. But it is hard to feel sympathetic towards a man who forces you naked onto the bed, rolls you onto your belly and whips your buttocks until they bleed, before continuing what he calls taking his wife in the manner he prefers.

"Undress," he now spat in my face. "Get those frivolities off, girl, and show yourself to me."

I hated undressing for him, but I always obeyed. I wasn't fully dressed yet so untying my ribbons wasn't too hard. Once I stood only in my petticoat, my knees trembling beneath, He ripped the thin linen off me, one clawed hand between my breasts, and without delay threw me back onto the bed. I collapsed there like a sack of tipsy but brainless flesh and bones, which is how he treated me. He slapped my legs and belly as he forced onto and into me, his rings scraping against me as he pummelled.

"Getting skinny," he muttered. "I want you plump. Eat more. I like a pudding arse like the suet crust on my dinner. Get eating, girl. Pudding up, or I'll shove the spoon down your throat myself."

I wasn't going to answer. Besides, I was gasping for breath. My thigh was bleeding and a growing headache pounded as hard as he did.

Nearly two months in bed had left me partially ignorant of the political situation around me. His majesty, convinced that he must act as he saw fit, needed the funds which parliament was refusing him. Charles had always been a man of confused ideals, convinced that as the Lord God's divine choice as sovereign of the country he had been born to, he must act as seemed right to him, and therefore Parliament's decisions were utterly irrelevant. They should simply agree with him and act as he demanded. Less arrogant than this made him seem, our wretched king felt duty bound to serve the god which had put him on the throne. As a boy, second in line to the crown, Charles had been a shy child, ashamed of his weaknesses and lack of height. He saw himself as a failure and a failure to his grand family.

And then the ridiculous occurred, for his elder brother Henry, the future king, died and left Charles to inherit. Astonished and depressed, Charles accepted what seemed a tragic mistake, until he realised that since the Lord God could not possibly make mistakes, there must be a reason for Charles to be king. And the only reason Charles could imagine, was how this would be a lesson to him, to make him grow strong, to become decisive, and to rule as a champion to God's church. He must no longer see himself as weak. He must see himself as invincible, and uphold everything the Bible preached. God had presented him with the ultimate duty, and his duty to the Lord was to fulfil the role hung so heavily around his neck.

And so Charles I was, perhaps the first crowned monarch who had never wanted the title, and yet became the rigid and unveiling tyrant so many of his people hated.

Poor little Charles.

Wretched little Arthur. Both feeling the stigma of stunted height and deep inner vulnerability. But whereas this led Arthur to the putrid behaviour I was forced to experience, Charles took on his duty and attempted to do his best. A fanatical and over-zealous duty, but one he thought did homage to the God he adored.

I also knew my duty and realised that I had to fight for him. I did not know Cromwell nor any other leading politician, but I knew the Puritan church and its ideals, and hated them. My husband, although the least moral creature I had ever known, rose to fight for parliament. I also hated that same infernal husband, which made everything simple.

I asked him, "Why, my lord, since you are a member of the

aristocracy, not the government, and you've never attended the puritan churches in your life?"

He actually had the grace to answer me and explain, although he hit me first. He knocked me into the fireplace, punching his closed fist at my mouth.

My bottom lip split and bled while my skirts scorched in the ashes. "You dare question me, wench?" he demanded, glaring.

I managed to scramble up before catching fire. "Never, my lord," I mumbled since I invariably gave the coward's answer. "But because I respect all your decisions, and so know this must be the right one, I hoped to understand why."

"What female would understand my reasoning?" the idiot said, but sat back, fanned out his lace cuffs, and began to explain. "The king does not support me, and I've no desire to support him. Besides, he wants the country's money to make war. A waste of coin, if you ask me. Blood is expensive, and we all want to keep our inheritance to ourselves. Cromwell, being a fool, will never win the argument, but he should teach the king a lesson, and keep him quiet for a year or more."

"It seems odd," I ventured, "that you want to fight on what you say you know is the losing side."

He paused, frowning. "Not that, not indeed. It shall be the winning side but without consequences," he eventually decided. "Cromwell will remain in parliament, then be voted out. But the king will have learned a lesson and shut his foolish mouth in future."

"I'm aware that you don't like his majesty, my lord." No one could miss it. Charles thought my husband a bad-tempered idiot, as of course he was. They had argued once, and Charles had called the guard to see Lord Harrington out. I wish they'd locked him up. But my putrid lord and master was an earl, a rich one, and escaped punishment. But he had never been invited to court since. Now he wanted some sort of revenge even though he had no idea whatsoever what Cromwell was fighting about. Nor would the vile man ever lift a sword or a musket, he'd simply shout from a safe distance.

So Lord Arthur, Earl of Harrington, joined the side of the commoners and puritans although he was neither commoner nor in any manner puritan.

Entirely unknown to him, I meanwhile joined the side of the royalists. Unable to arm myself, choose one of the destriars from our stables, clamp on my helmet and my sword, or take up my musket and ride to battle, I offered my services in a very different way. First speaking to her highness, the royal consort, Queen Henrietta, we discussed the limited possibilities. From there, she took me to his majesty and although he remained rigid, unimaginative, and concerned over the rightful place of a lady in society, we finally each managed concessions, and I became a spy for the king.

"Cromwell has a whole network of spies," I informed his majesty.

"How unlikely," King Charles shook his royal brow.

There was no point arguing since I knew I was right and he would never accept a woman arguing with him anymore than my husband would. Men were the masters of course.

No musket after all. But as half the time they blew off the gunman's hand anyway, exploded in his face, or simply took so long to reload that someone else would hack him to death in the meantime, I didn't care. However, combining my lack of experience with the king's lack of most other things, it was some time before I could manage serious work.

Arthur, on the other hand, did nothing whatsoever, but proclaimed his belief in the puritan side. I refrained from ever informing him what he should, or should not, be doing. Every detail of his behaviour was of course in absolute contradiction to the Puritan beliefs.

His absurd conversion to the Puritan cause helped me enormously. Knowing him to be a supporter of Cromwell, the people assumed that my own loyalties were to the same side. A good number of the aristocracy turned against the king's intolerance, so we did not seem suspicious. And I, good little Puritan, wore modest clothes and went to visit the members of parliament at Cromwell's side. Some were ardent, some puzzled, many were religious but a majority simply disliked the arrogance of a king seeing himself as God-sent, impossible ever to see himself as wrong, or even consider a compromise with the comfort of his people. Besides, the queen was an immovable Catholic, and that was a problem indeed. So I sat at tables both huge and tiny, eating both feasts and pitiful scraps, speaking with those who battled our monarch. Some of these men knew a good deal concerning Cromwell's future intentions, and were prepared to discuss them even with a woman.

Then, with as much secrecy as I could manage, I went to the king's senior officers and told my stories. Whether this had any relevance or brought even the slightest benefit to his majesty, I have no idea. Less, I think, than it should have. I was often disbelieved. Many of the king's chief officers were as immovably intolerant as he was.

When I met the man Jasper, I was unprepared. A tall man, he was striding Cromwell's camp, a musket stuck through his belt and the wind through his hair. No wig, and his clothes were plain, although they did not follow the puritan fashion, nor was he especially handsome. Yet something about his face sang to me. His arrogance, perhaps. Did I have a fascination for the arrogance of many men, considering both my husband and my king? This was a far taller man than either of those, but his arrogance spilled from those cold black eyes, and his mouth neither lifted nor relaxed. Actually, I bumped into him, which was no mistake. I managed to lose my balance at the correct moment, and attempted to tumble into his arms. Unfortunately, he saw the stagger in time, and avoided the damsel in distress. Seeing me, however, he bowed as I staggered upright, and apologised for being in the way. Civil, but absurd.

I had thought that if I might gain from talking to someone on the enemy side, then it might as well be someone interesting. This man's eyes were like the cruel hooks where butcher's hang their meat. And I was hooked. When he walked onwards without a single glance in my direction, I was both disappointed and cross.

Three days later I saw him again. This time I had arranged nothing, and was on horseback, heading back into London over the Bridge, and clomped up towards Cheapside, my page on the pony behind me. Not much of a security guard, but all I wanted or thought I needed. The other horse was coming in the opposite direction and stopped directly in front of me. The rider bowed, and removed his hat. I already knew who he was since there was no one else like him.

"My lady," he said very softly, "it appears we are fated to become acquainted."

His voice held inner strength, but it was so quiet, I had to strain to hear him. I was, however, delighted that he remembered me. I smiled and said, "I have no idea who you are, sir. You must tell me your name."

Improper, I knew. But who cared? I just wanted to get to know him. He'd be an excellent source of information for my spying, and I knew I'd enjoy his company.

He bowed even though he remained in his saddle and replaced his hat.

"I am Jasper Fairweather, my lady," he said, "A common man of no consequence. Yet in spite of the lack of title and the even greater lack of propriety, under such circumstances, I shall be delight to know your own name, madam."

The soft voice again. But I heard every word and answered with a smile.

"The Lady Sarah Harrington, sir," I told him, and called him sir even though he wasn't one. I wanted friendship. "And the last time I saw you, we were both in a compromised situation. Now we are simply passing each other on the street and cannot be accused of anything."

"Except that of a common man introducing himself to a high-born lady, with no previous knowledge of each other to excuse the impertinence."

I spoke as quickly as I could. "But we are now old friends, Master Fairweather, and there is therefore no impropriety should I suggest that you escort me to The Turk's Head where we can share the new fashion of coffee mixed with politics.

It's not far from here, I believe."

His mouth twitched just on one side, a half-hearted smile of acceptance. Whether disguised reluctance or disguised eagerness, I wasn't at all sure. But the coffee house was not far off, and he seemed to know the way. Only minutes on horseback. I'd never yet been there and had wanted to for several months. No point asking my husband of course.

The candles were spitting and kept the corners dark. Privacy could be important in such a newly introduced place of dubious reputation. There had been talk of banning both the drink and the place of its preparation, but so far, we were legal even if definitely improper. But Jasper spoke to the proprietor, and we were instantly shown to one of the corner tables, tiny and uncovered, with two cushions seats. I shuffled into the darkness, and once I was cosy and well tucked in, he sat facing me. The coffee itself was a vile concoction and as black as mud with a taste about the same. But the conversation was quite another matter.

"A place of instant friendship," said my new friend. "How," he paused, then said, "interesting."

I giggled, which wasn't something I usually did. Actually, I despised gigglers, and here I was, embarrassed into doing just what I disliked. "I expect," I said, keeping my voice down, "you've been to this place before. They call it a house of sin, but it isn't, is it."

"I imagine," he answered, "that such places will become quite numerous in the future. Personally, I cannot see how coffee contains any particular sin, nor is the meeting of those who drink it. If anything, I would be more likely to criticise the tavern or the ale house. Although perhaps not under Cromwell's judgement since he enjoys labelling life as sinful. I happen to enjoy the drinking of coffee which directly proves that Cromwell will not."

I felt that real future popularity was most unlikely, but didn't say so. Instead I said, "Well, Master Fairweather, perhaps we should discuss politics since we met in unusual circumstances, and it seems that we both support the same side."

And at that he really did smile. A proper smile. And he said, "It would seem so, my lady. Although I am not entirely sure which side that might be."

CHAPTER ELEVEN

I told Vespasian that he was a flirt, and he laughed at me.

"Flirting with my wife is a sin, perhaps?"

"Sarah's a complete stranger," I objected. "And she's no way your wife because I am."

"And she is you, my love," he grinned.

"But she's married to Arthur Harrington," I pointed out. "He's seriously disgusting of course. She'd love to have you instead. But even if she is me, she can't have you."

I was curled beside him on the rug before the fire, cosy but conscious of the unguarded flames. The cottage we had bought stood in cheap little Hammersmith, no longer a street of smiths hammering into the evening, but an overcrowded village with cheap rooms to rent and a sky of thick black smoke from the chimneys. The river pushed past the cottage we'd taken, dark as the smoke and stinking of faeces and decay. A minute bedchamber, a trivet over the fire for cooking, and a living room the size of a hamburger. But we had added our own special touches and what Vespasian did when he felt like it, was always astonishing. Besides, our cottage sat alone without close neighbours, and I soon adored it. Oh, that bed. And Vespasian's arms, instead of the mud and snivelling puritan wives awaiting their husbands, all drunk of course as they celebrated their victories.

My possessive words clearly didn't bother Vespasian in the slightest. "My dearest beloved," he said with faint amusement, "we are come to destroy demons and not to fuck the enemy."

"You don't really think she's the enemy," I pointed out, since he knew very well that she was a royalist spy. "Is she pretty?"

"Yes, she is," he nodded without hesitation. "Yet does not resemble you except for a faint familiarity within the eyes. And she is the same height, although not the same width."

So he'd looked close and certainly noticed a lot. "Oh well," I sighed, "she can't be as nice as me. Nobody is."

Kissing down the side of my neck, his breath was as warm as the fire. "Naturally true, my delicious angel," he said between kisses. "But you should accustom yourself to the fact that she is you, and you are her, and there is no other person between you."

I knew it of course. When I slipped into Sarah's mind, I was at first conscious of my own thoughts and knowledge as well as hers. I had done the same long ago with Tilda. Yet, once I slid deeper into Sarah's mind, I was her alone, and modern Molly disappeared. A brief lurking hint of something unnatural sometimes remained as though I was half asleep and dreaming, but even this was rare. Sarah, after all, was a very determined young woman and although she had learned to be weak and obedient to her husband, inside she brooded and practised her own strength.

It took Sarah only two short weeks to realise that she was in love – or perhaps in lust – with my husband.

Well, that was something we could certainly both agree on.

Vespasian, on the other hand, claimed that apart from a vague veneer of curiosity, what he needed was an introduction to the horrible husband, for the principal demon was enthroned there, and gaining strength. Cromwell's inner problem was equally urgent since his actions affected more than a few people, but there did not exist a friendship close enough for action.

"We're mad," I told Vespasian. "Utterly crazy. We've travelled time and space to tackle demons from our own garden and ended up with the problem of me meeting me."

"I find the duplication of the woman I love to be a charming and fascinating circumstance," Vespasian smiled at me, each corner of his mouth tucked, and eyelids lowered. I gazed back. I thought his statement was both flattering and insulting. "Yet," he continued, "the meeting of your two incarnations would be unwise."

"One would disappear?" I shivered.

But he was still smiling. "No," He was running his fingers through my hair as though untangling knots. No decent hairbrush and plenty of wind meant my hair tangled constantly. "You, my beloved, being the one out of your life's time progression, would begin to fade. Returning to your modern state would reinstate you. But the complication would be difficult to explain."

"I won't meet her."

"You, little one, will stay close to Agnes Oats."

She was the last person I wanted to stay close to, but it was what I had come for, and would be my safest path.

CHAPTER TWELVE

With the stink of his breath in my mouth and the clamp of his fingers on my neck, I wanted to follow the habit of several years and whisper, *Yes, my lord,* and *Whatever you wish, my lord.* Yet I searched my head for the courage I fostered in the years of my youth, and managed a quivering denial.

"I swear it, my lord, I have never been disloyal and never unfaithful. I would never cuckold the man I respect and admire. I have only met this other man, a common man who follows Cromwell with all his heart, twice and both times without intention or appointment. It is you, my lord, who this man wishes to know, and not myself at all."

Lies, hypocrisy and cowardly nonsense. But it was also practical and therefore worked whereas any admittance closer to the truth might have finished me entirely.

The snarl remained, but Arthur released my throat. I could breathe and I quickly stepped back. His spit, however, still splattered my face as he spoke. "And how do you know this gutter scraping isn't some royalist assassin in disguise?"

What a sweet thought. "He is neither a creature of the gutter nor an assassin, sir. He speaks with Cromwell in their camp and is often seen with him. His clothes are of quality, and he rides a fine horse."

Snarling again. "You know so much about him? It's a lie, then, that you've met him only twice."

I shrank back again. "No lie, my lord. But I have seen him many times in the camps, yet without meeting the man or speaking with him. I know only that he's a true supporter of our cause, a gentleman if not a lord of title, and that he wishes to meet and speak with you. He admires you, so wishes to talk with you."

Finally, the loathsome creature relaxed, stood back and began to wander over to the table where the wine decanter stood. He poured himself a glass but didn't offer me one. Then he nodded and said, "Then bring the fool over one day. You see him often enough, so make an appointment. Clear it with me first, then bring him for midday dinner. I'll permit it."

I ran upstairs and collapsed on the bed. Even such a small matter became a terrifying encounter when it involved Arthur. But for once, I'd succeeded.

It was six days before I saw Jasper Fairweather again, and he didn't notice me at first. I had to wait until he'd finished speaking with the small group of Cromwell's men, and then sidle over in the hope he wouldn't just walk away.

He didn't. He stood before me and smiled down at my blushes. "Sir, you once told me you wished to meet my husband," I reminded him. "Is that still what you want?" I didn't add that no one else in the entire world ever wanted to meet with Arthur, Lord Harrington, the beast of Bracken House first house on the road to Hell.

"Then I am suitably delighted, my lady," he said, bowing dutifully. "Has a suitable time been arranged?"

I said no, and hoped he'd suggest that we discuss the matter once again at the coffee shop. Sadly, he did not. I said, "You are formally invited to Bracken House at midday to share our dinner, sir. But the day is for you to choose, since I presume you are a busy man. I shall then confirm the date with my lord."

"Then it must be next week," said the man. "Tuesday at midday would be convenient, but Wednesday would be equally suitable."

And damn the man, he just walked off. Another bow, another smile, and his boots disappearing over the hillocks and the mud. I stood there quite bereft, and then made my own cross departure.

Arthur had to be difficult, and so the chosen day was denied, but he agreed to the following Wednesday. I was delighted. I hurried to the lodgings in the city where the government's top men usually gathered to discuss all and every situation, plot and programme. The man I wanted was there. I was invited in since half the men knew me already and had seen me often, and there, next to the window, Jasper Fairweather sat, long legs stretched, ankles crossed, elbow resting on the arm of the chair and his chin on his knuckles as he gazed at the rain outside.

I was soggy and dripped as I stumbled in and approached him. "Sir," I said in a rush, "you are invited to our home next Wednesday to take our midday meal with us, and Lord Harrington will be delighted to greet you, sir."

It was agreed without surprise.

And indeed, my husband met him at the door. Oh, my good Lord, what a contrast. Jasper stood straight, no wig, with his rich black hair brushed back and somewhat longer than the Puritan fashion now favoured. He carried his hat and gloves, and wore dark clothes, fine white lace cravat and cuffs below the dark brown jacket, long boots and no rings or other decorations. But he was no strict Puritan, that was clear.

My husband reached only to Jasper's shoulder, but was dressed in every ribbon, every golden ornament and every piece of satin and lace he owned. Whereas Jasper showed no Puritan values, Arthur clearly displayed a desire to show off both wealth and status. His new wig, long and heavily curled, was russet and did not suit him at all. Beneath, his own hair, although now shaved to discourage the latest swarm of head lice, was a limp brown.

Oh yes, the food was carefully planned too – with linen and lace, silver and glassware. Three different soups, a huge crusted pie of venison cooked in red wine, and served with onions and parsnips, roast pheasant with beans cooked in spices, blackberry jellies with cream and a lemon tart served with custard. With lavish generosity there was also Spanish Jerez as well as wine, and sugar-coated biscuits. It was the best feast I'd eaten since my wretched wedding day, and I ate a good deal of everything, and drank everything too, much to Arthur's obvious disgust. I didn't like the Jerez, but I drank it all the same since I knew it had cost a fortune.

Our guest was not so hungry, and he ate only roast pheasant and drank only wine. I'm not sure whether Arthur was delighted or disappointed at this. After all, he'd made his grand splash and yet enough food remained to keep us well fed for a week and still have something left over for the staff.

"I have been hoping to meet you, my lord Harrington," Jasper said quietly. "I am no fanatical Puritan myself, but believe in Cromwell's cause. I understand that you feel exactly the same way."

"Do I? Yes, of course," said my idiot husband. "The church is none of my concern. The politics, however, are a matter of considerable urgency, sir. I shall be pleased to hear your opinion."

Leaning back in his chair and raising his glass of wine, Jasper did not glance once at me. "England does not require a king who believes himself beyond criticism," he said in his usual soft murmur. "The French have suffered from the holy idealism of the monarchy for too long, and now it has rebounded to us, even though under the Tudor Queen Elizabeth, the sovereign, if not the church, became a more tolerant affair. Her successor James, however, believed that tolerance was a weakness. Now his son Charles is too impressed by his title. Cromwell has a more charitable intention."

"Ah yes," Arthur said, gulping. "A gentle and trustworthy gentleman."

My guest smiled. "I'd call him neither, my lord, and since I know him fairly well, I'd say he has not a gentle bone in his body. Yet his ideals for the country are well intentioned, and some changes will be well managed."

"A principled gentleman," Arthur was tipsy enough to permit himself corrected.

I'd be scalded for it afterwards, but now I interrupted. "He is no gentleman," I said. "And he believes in a god who cares only to deny his people any form of peaceful and harmless entertainment."

Turning on me with the accustomed snarl, Arthur hiccupped and then shouted, "You sound like a royalist, shameful bigoted female. And since you know nothing of politics, nor of anything else except the cost of your petticoats, you will keep silent while I speak with Master Fairweather."

Having blushed scarlet from embarrassment and shame, I would have done as I was told and kept utterly silent, but Jasper turned to me. "On the contrary," he said in that soft chant of his, "I happen to agree with much you say, my lady, for Cromwell's beliefs are morally fanatical, and I do not agree that our Lord would be angry with any man or woman who sang like the birds, or wore clothes as bright as the sunset. The Lord God has fashioned his world in ornate beauty, and if we follow His example, then I cannot see the sin."

"Humph," said Arthur, quickly refilling his wine glass with Jerez and his sherry glass with wine.

"Yet perhaps his majesty is too autocratic," I mumbled, and again Jasper answered me.

"He misunderstands the duty of a leader, he misunderstands duty, and he misunderstands justice," Jasper said. "Whereas Cromwell attempts a more hospitable justice which includes the common man, and sees no benefit in constant wars abroad where we gain nothing but lose our lives and our monetary security." He filled my wine glass for me and passed it across the table. Arthur sat at the head, myself on his left and Jasper on his right. Therefore, Jasper and I faced each other. "It is wise, I believe to see the rights and the wrongs in those you support as well as in those who rage against you."

I nodded, although the one who raged against me was always my damned husband, and I saw no right in him at all. Actually, I thought he might fall off his chair. I had never personally ever seen him so intoxicated. If I called his valet and commanded that the lord be taken up to his bed, it would have been perfect. But I couldn't dare arrange that unless the wretched creature fell flat on his face.

Jasper cheerfully refilled Arthur's sherry glass, and since the other crystal had been muddled, he used the water tumbler. This was considerably larger. I began to wonder if he had the same motives I had myself.

It was an hour later when Jasper indicated to one of the staff that he wished to rise. His chair was drawn back for him, and he stood, once again addressing the befuddled lord of the house. "I wonder, my lord," he said, "whether you would care to take a walk with me in the garden?"

"Yush, yush," said my husband brightly. "Letsh go." Scraping back the chair, it toppled backwards and himself with it. Tumbling directly onto his back, he lay there on the carpet, waved one hand, and closed his eyes.

"Are you alright, my lord?" inquired the soft voice.

"Yush, tush," Arthur mumbled between hiccups. "Shtay here. All show huppy." His eyes closed again, and he began to snore.

The staff crowded around. "Call Robinson," I commanded. "Then carry his lordship to bed." With a quick smile at Jasper, I suggested, "I will be pleased to accompany you on that walk in the garden, sir, should you wish it and clearly my husband is unable to oblige."

"I should be delighted," the expected answer.

Our grounds were neither minute nor huge, an average space for a grand house I supposed, with gravel paths and hillocks of grass. The sun was ebbing but still shone as it hovered over the rooftop horizon. I wrapped my shawl around my shoulders, and Jasper followed me out onto the paved terrace, and stood there, looking across to the west. Then oblivious to any of the staff who might be watching, I hooked my arm into Jasper's, and began to walk. I knew exactly which direction I aimed towards, but explained nothing and simply chatted about the weather, the price of spices, the politics concerning puritan insistence on dark plain colours, and the king's younger brother, whom I disliked.

"The king may have ideas which seem arrogant," I mumbled, "but in fact that's his attempt at fulfilling his duty. His brother, on the other hand, is truly arrogant and is quite sure he'll make a better king."

Jasper seemed only vaguely interested in any of my mutterings, although he did once reply, "My dear Sarah, this is not the usual opinion expressed by Cromwell's followers. You should be careful who you address in such a manner. And are you, I wonder, prepared for the king's execution, should such a thing come to pass?"

Only one part of this interested me, and that was when he'd called me his dear Sarah. Previously it had always been Lady Harrington. I probably smirked, but simply said, "I doubt it will come to that, since Cromwell would neither dare such a thing, nor gain the opportunity."

The tiny summerhouse was little more than a roofed archway overlooking an artificial pond. Yet within the three stone corners, the shadows played as a streak of sunshine crossed towards the daybed. Designed for two lovers to lay in the summer's warmth yet relish the shade, this was a wide chair stretching into a mattressed cocoon. And as we came close, I pointed.

"Shall we rest while we talk, Master Jasper?"

I didn't permit him to refuse, and walked the two steps into the faint perfume of briar roses and warm air.

Now standing in the shadows, I turned to face him. He was leaning against the wall and watching me, thumbs in his belt and his ankles crossed. Perhaps he knew what I was going to do.

"You called me your dear Sarah," I said quickly. "May I address you as my dear Jasper?"

As usual I had to strain to hear his voice. "You may call me as you wish," he murmured, "and Jasper is my name, little one."

So I stood there next to the day bed with my knees like water, biting my lip and wondering if this was the biggest mistake of my life. Then I decided that I was going to do it anyway, mistake or otherwise, and I began to unlace the top of my gown from beneath my arm. It was a bit of a struggle without my maids, but Jasper didn't help. He just stood completely silent and completely unmoving. But he watched me from beneath heavy lids, eyes narrowed, continuing to breathe without tension or any sign of either delight or disapproval.

Then I was naked to the waist, shivered a moment, slowly turned and lit the one little candle on the stool beside the day bed. Immediately the tiny flicker of flame reflected in his eyes. He didn't blink. So I sat carefully on the day bed, swung up my legs and clasped my hands in my lap. I faced him and waited.

"A woman's breasts," he murmured, even more softly than before, "follow an individual curve which she alone can claim to own. The delight, to a man, is when that gentle curve is shown just to him, and he knows its unique beauty. When making love to a woman, he feels that intimacy to be the most glorious he has ever known. Yet the next experience will be the same, and each after that. Love making brings love, however momentary."

He paused, and I swallowed, waiting. Then I whispered into the pause. "Make love to me then, Jasper." I knew my breasts were quivering, but he wasn't even breathing faster.

One step, then two, and he stood over me, then sat half beside me, half facing. His fingers were long and hard tipped as a man used to the notching of the arrow, the grasping of the sword hilt, and the clutch to the reins of a horse. He slid one finger softly down the side of my breast and around over the nipple, then beneath. Finally, he said, "Your breasts are beautiful. Their curve is high and heavy, and sings directly to the tightness in my groin." He was looking into my eyes, and not at where his fingers were. "I might make love to you, little one, and satisfy us both. Tonight, perhaps I shall dream of what I failed to do," he continued. "But I came here today for your husband and for no other reason, and I shall not twice take such callous advantage of his condition."

He was saying no. I didn't understand the rest. But I leaned my head over on his shoulder and started to cry. I couldn't help it. I felt such a blithering fool, so ugly and so stupid, and my sobs were soaking his cravat.

He moved me back a little, lifting my chin with his fingers. And then I realised that it was his tongue which licked my tears away. Hot breath in my ear and then his murmur, "But it is your husband I came for, my dear, and I will neither take advantage of your loneliness, nor take advantage of my wife's particular ability to understand. For it is my wife I adore, little one, and your – let us say – likeness to her, does not excuse my attraction." And he leaned forwards, helping me hoist up the straps of my petticoats, kissed my forehead very lightly, and murmured, "Forgive me. But I shall not complicate what is already so vastly complicated."

As he helped me dress, I quickly realised how practised he was with a woman's clothes. And when I was once again respectable, he took my hand and began to walk back to the house. The sun had set and the hundred windows staring back at us were ablaze with candlelight. Above us the sky was darkening from the grey stupor to black night and the first stars were blinking out as we entered the house.

CHAPTER THIRTEEN

J asper said, "Take me to your husband's bedchamber," and I
did. Up the stairs and along the corridor to the master's
chamber at the front of the house, overlooking the grand
entrance. The door was a little ajar, and Arthur's snores
rebounded.

I pushed in. The chamber was dark and no candle was lit, but
with the bed curtains open and the window shutters down,
moonlight striped the bed. My husband lay deeply asleep, eyes
firmly shut and mouth gaping open. No one had undressed him
but his long jacket was unfastened, his cravat removed, his belt
flung aside and the fastenings on the waist of his knee length
britches had been undone. His legs were splayed, no shoes, and
stockings wrinkled. I thought he looked even more hideous than
usual. I wondered what on earth Jasper intended doing with him
and all I could think of was that he wished to kill the man.

Was I supposed to comply? Was I expected to help? What I
had so stupidly done in the summer house, and how Jasper had
not at first stopped me, did not arouse my distrust. But I
reminded myself I did not know the man however much I loved

him. Now I simply stood by, controlling my nervousness, and watched.

Jasper sat on the bed beside Arthur and stared down at him. Then he bent over him like a hungry wolf, clasping Arthur's head between both palms. At once Jasper started to whisper words I didn't understand. I could only grasp a few. For a man whose voice was always quiet, now it was just a breeze in the night.

He said the muffled sounds of, "Diabulus, nio relinque, lacrimo neoquarm," and my husband began to tremble.

I stood back. I was not asked to help, nor to leave so I stood and stared. I could see that Jasper was not hurting anyone, and his hands were spread quite gently to either side of Arthur's head. Much as I loathed my husband, his death now would have been obvious murder with the risk of where the blame might be attached. The lurch of guilt, since clearly, I had no real objection to his sudden death, didn't even last long. But not murder after all. Indeed, not anything I could understand. I stood like an idiot, clasping my shawl and sniffing. This all continued so I sat on the opposite side of the bed and tried to listen.

The murmur of strange words ground on, and Arthur began to flail. I began to think he was waking, but that wasn't it. His eyes not only remained shut, but seemed glued. Yet his arms were flung upwards by some sleeping impulse and his legs thrashed. Since his britches were already undone and the belt thrown off, he was soon almost undressed and the small bent legs kicked. He rolled over, then back. And as he turned, laying suddenly calm, his eyes snapped open. But they weren't Arthur's eyes.

They were greener than the spring grass and as vivid as a man wide awake. He wasn't interested in me of course. He stared at Jasper. But now I was quite sure that whoever he was, he wasn't my husband.

The new voice was so unpleasant, I thought it crueller than ever Arthur's had been. The thing's words grated like small forced coughs and sounded like knife thrusts. "You have no power over me," it said.

Jasper spoke English, and I could understand him again. "Leave the essence," he said, this time loud and clear.

The other voice cackled. "My essence, absurd human. No man can force me out, not even the one I suck."

"You do not know my power, nor do you know my intentions. As Lilith lost all power, so she disintegrated into the ether and pissed out all the fragments of her evil. Now each fragment believes itself divine, and feeds on others, each cannibalising its companion in order to grow stronger. So will you feed or will you be the food of another. Will you feel yourself chewed like nuts on the bush, and be swallowed into the abyss of another's evil?"

"When I have sucked this human dry," said the rasping screech, "I shall move to another and take it until I am the strongest in this world of men."

"Every fragment of cruelty has its limits."

I saw something flicker over Arthur's head. A shadowed green, murky and stained as though leaking its own body mass. I thought it spoke with its eyes. They darted and glowed, then shrank back into the hollows of the face.

Jasper told the thing, "You understand only cruelty, yet crudelitatem crudelitatemque - stultitia - erit semper resiliant." Now even his voice had changed. This felt like a chant, a little like the chanting in church which I had once loved, and the thing I had seen within my husband, now crawled back. I was shivering again and twisted my fingers so tightly together, they began to hurt and then felt numb.

With an abrupt lurch, my husband opened his own dark eyes, stared around, grabbed his own head and screamed, "Help. Help me." His wig had fallen uncovering his small shaved head, leaving only the stubs of greasy hair, and now he clawed his scalp, screaming, "Get it out. Get it out now. I command you to help me."

"I have indeed been helping," Jasper said, his voice soft once more. "But now you have woken far too soon, my lord, and no doubt your servants are running to your call. I shall therefore escort Lady Harrington to the salon downstairs, and order supper to be made ready for her. I shall then leave, my lord, and hope to see you again on a more salubrious occasion."

I almost laughed and then I almost collapsed. Finally, I trotted meekly downstairs with Jasper. I could hear Arthur's valet, head page and barber dashing into his chamber, begging to know what was wrong and how they could help. My own head was in a whirl, and I was wondering how dangerous Jasper might be. I followed as he marched into the living room, stood looking down at the empty grate, his elbow to the mantel and his back to me.

I sat and waited.

It was quite some time before he turned at last. His eyes were once again cold, heavy lidded and unblinking.

"Come here," he said.

And then I was afraid of him all over again. I imagined myself broken between his hands, as though I was shattered crockery.

Yet, obedient as usual, I stood and stepped slowly towards him. He didn't speak again. He waited, unmoving and without any expression, until I stood directly in front of him and as close as I dared.

Abruptly he clasped the back of my shoulders, both hands tight, and pulled me close. Then he turned me and suddenly pressed me back against the wall next to the fireplace, leaned hard against me and kissed me on the mouth, so harshly he almost bit. I felt my lips forced open and the heat of his breath down my throat. His eyes remained open, almost crimson with the candle flame's refection, unblinking and as fierce as the thing he forced out from my husband.

But I closed my eyes and breathed in his breath. His hands crawled, one up to the back of my head with his fingers in my hair, and the other hand down to the back of my waist, and inching further to where he should not have touched.

Sudden again, as abrupt as the kiss, Jasper released me. I rocked back, dizzy and unbalanced. He sighed and spoke again.

"I shall in no way harm you," he murmured in that breeze-soft voice, "And as I speak to you now, I am speaking directly to my wife. That will seem absurd to you, but I will not attempt explanations. That would not serve my purpose, since I come not for you, my dear, but to bring out the force of evil from your husband. Once that is done, as it shall be soon enough, I shall explain as you wish."

I whispered back, "So do you want anything from me?"

"You know exactly what I want from you," he said without obvious emotion. "My desire to discover you further and explore your own needs is as strong as I permit it. But I will not come to your bed. I shall, instead, bring you what you need far more, which is the peace and the freedom to be yourself, and to discover the husband who may bring you satisfaction and tranquillity. That shall be either Arthur Harrington transformed, or another man for you to meet in the future."

Longing now and wanting more time, all absurd fear dissolved, I spoke quickly before he could leave. "You didn't finish," I mumbled. "Arthur, I mean. What is it? The thing inside? Demons, or something else?" I looked down, knowing I'd blush scarlet if I saw him watching me. "Arthur is a cruel man," I whispered. "He – hurts me. Purposefully. He has mistresses of course, but I don't know them so I can't ask if he hurts them too. I think he probably does because he doesn't seem to get – satisfaction – without perverse – behaviour."

It was all in a fast gabble, and I half expected Jasper to move away, revolted. But he did the opposite, and drew me close to him, one hand against the back of my head.

"You are stronger than you appear to know," he told me gently. "You have the courage to push this creature away. Yes, he houses demons. A demon which has already absorbed others. The number is unimportant. What is important is your own will to protect yourself."

"No one can fight a husband,' I sniffed. "Would you let your wife tell you no?"

I saw him smile and was surprised. "A secret joke," he told me. "And the answer is most certainly yes, my dear. Protect yourself as you can, and don't fear this man. I shall take out the demon when I can, and it will not be long now. But in the meantime, my dear Sarah, prove your strength to yourself."

He moved away, called to the page to bring his hat, gloves and coat, shrugged them on, and bowed. "My lady, I shall return when I can." And he swept out from the room so quickly that I hardly knew what had happened.

Flopping back down onto the large chair by the empty grate, I struggled to remember everything he'd done and everything he'd said, and sat shaking, desperate to regain my balance. I wondered if it was a dream. I couldn't eat the supper now served to me. But when I staggered upstairs with the intention of collapsing early to bed, I heard my husband call.

Reluctantly, I went to him. Arthur was in a nightshirt, tucked up beneath his eiderdown, but wide awake. I stared, and wished it was a different man I was staring at.

"Yes, my lord? You have been unwell," I said flatly. "You seemed to have drunk too much at midday, or perhaps the content did not agree with you. I trust you now feel better?"

He was staring with a puzzled belligerence. "I never drink too much. No, I must have been poisoned."

"Unlikely, my lord. No royalist spies work in our kitchens, I assure you."

Without the accusation that he suspected me, I relaxed and sat, hands in lap, on the bedside chair. He scowled at me. "Get me wine, now. And make sure it isn't poisoned."

Jasper's words came back into my head, and I breathed in courage as he'd told me. "Your page and valet were here until moments past," I pointed out. "Why didn't you send one of them for wine? I cannot become your servant, my lord."

Well, I had been his servant since we married, but I risked speaking now since he was safe tucked in bed.

His scowl deepened. "They brought me nothing as the doctor advised me not to touch alcohol for two days. But wine is harmless. I don't ask for Jerez."

He was clutching at his head. "You have a headache, sir?" He should have the worst headache of his life after all the drinking and then the thing inside.

Nodding, Arthur lay back. "Willow tonic then. To kill the pain. I'll sleep well enough, I imagine." And he shut his eyes.

When they brought him the willow bark medicine, I left him alone and hurried to my own room. The maid had warmed my bed, but it felt icy cold and so empty.

I tried very hard to dream off the kiss and those dark tunnel eyes, but instead I dreamed of green-eyed wraiths and a harsh disembodied voice screeching of power and cruelty.

CHAPTER FOURTEEN

I'd lived through Sarah's excitement, her horror and disgust, and then the galloping awakenment of her desire for my Vespasian. As Sarah, I'd wanted him so deeply, agonising for the experience of sweet love making. Having only ever experienced Arthur Harrington's perverted cruelty, my poor Sarah-self didn't even really know what lovemaking meant.

But back in myself as Molly again, I didn't want Vespasian to sleep with another woman, even though she was me. And would he actually be making love to me – or to her – and would he think it was the same thing – or would he admire a different body even when he knew he was talking to the inner me.

Oh bother. Muddled nonsense of course. I swallowed it back and said nothing to my own Jasper Fairweather.

Instead, he said it to me, "Your eyes yearned. I saw you, my dearest, within the woman I touched. It was you I wished to take into my bed, as I knew it was you, my own precious beloved, when I had loved Tilda and then found you in my future. You are Tilda, and Sarah is you. This, even for me, is a delight I cannot entirely scrutinise with both heart and brain. I shall, perhaps, avoid you when you are not you, little one."

That made me laugh. "When I'm in Sarah, you could make love to me and I would love you back. But then you might make love to Sarah when I am only Molly, and can only guess what you are doing, I think that would hurt. Is that so stupid?"

And he nuzzled my neck. "I love only you, heart-born. And that will continue for the rest of my life, wherever I find you – in the body of another – of a queen – a pirate – or a lost soul needing comfort."

"I know you kissed me when you kissed Sarah," I smiled. "Because I was there. And I know Sarah loves you because I love you, and I'm her. But understanding these things is impossible, just like understanding you."

Instead I strode out to find Agnes Oats once more. I'd not seen her for days, and the camp where we'd met had packed up and moved on. Agnes would no doubt be back home, or sitting by another campfire further south.

Within the warm shadows of our thatched cottage, sitting on the outskirts of the village of Hammersmith, we had skipped time, Vespasian and I, a few harsh months blinked by in seconds as I lay in his arms in our new little cottage. He blinked and time blinked. Months had gone in that blink. But there was leisure when we wished it, to make love. And that was truly me as I lay in his arms and traced his nakedness as he traced mine.

Once awake, we strode out, ready to take our places in this wretched old world again.

From Hammersmith, I walked out towards the distant village of shepherd's Bush, and was delighted to discover the sheep on the green, and the shepherd's still active.

"That wretched Charles," spat the man walking near to me, "made peace with France only because he can't afford war. He fines his friends to get more coin, and rages against parliament because they won't agree to his demands. Thinks he's a god on earth, he does. Thinks he can make Scotland and Wales all one country with us English. But we don't want 'em. The man should be strung up for the magpies to pick at his eyes. Well, now the bugger's a prisoner. I hope they makes him pay."

I had begun to wonder if the entire population on both sides were occupied by these wretched demons since cruelty was like a bargaining tool, or a crazy dream of justice. Kindness was thought to achieve nothing.

It was a schoolhouse a little further north, and I knew Agnes Oats lived somewhere here. Asking for her had ended with an invitation to the school. The plump teacher Henry Bloom accepted my Puritan views and asked me to see where he taught, and where the pupils would learn true Christianity. I was supposed to be firmly on the side of Cromwell, and couldn't argue. Besides, what good would it do? This was four hundred years ago. I could hardly change the course of the great English Rebellion nor the bitter reformation that followed it. So I looked at the man sitting next to me at the table. "You uphold Puritan values? Is murder and torture God's will?"

"The Lord God? Ain't easy to understand. Murdered his own son, didn't he! But for the good of the people. Same with this useless king. Kill him off for the good of the people."

I sighed and stuffed the pork crackling into my mouth. The best part of a rather soggy dinner, since the only other choice was cabbage broth.

Scotland had rebelled when pushed into following the ideals of the church Charles believed was the only one. With pomp and circumstance claiming a major part of the High Anglican philosophy, the people accused Charles of returning to Catholicism. And Charles wanted this practised in Scotland, England and Wales. Scotland rebelled. Fighting against rebellions cost money. The parliament refused to grant it. Charles had promptly dissolved parliament.

But none of that mattered anymore, for Charles I, King of England, had been taken, imprisoned, and accused of treachery.

His son Charles had escaped. Stories concerning that abounded, and Henry Bloom, Agnes, the other teachers and I sat side by side on the wooden bench before the dining table eating left-over pork and cabbage broth and discussing what we thought comprised the rightful path for the future. We also discussed these exaggerated possibilities of how Prince Charles, heir to the throne, had escaped the country and Cromwell's committed soldiers.

"On a witches' broomstick I'd guess," frowned Henry.

"They say he hid in a tree," I suggested, being the only story I'd personally heard.

"I heard he sat astride a swan, and flew to France," said another teacher earnestly.

"Stuck 'is pitchfork up Cromwell's arse," sniggered Agnes.

"He was helped by that ungrateful royalist Rochester," Henry Bloom continued. "They'll make the fellow a baron or an earl, wait and see,"

I knew that the now exiled Prince Charles, the rightful heir, would return in just a few years and be welcomed as king and crowned. But I supposedly followed the parliamentary cause, and said nothing.

"Our so-called monarch? He'll be on trial by the end of the week and by the weekend, he'll swing on the gallows."

I sighed. "Master Bloom, surely he'll be beheaded. Not hanged."

Henry Bloom snorted into his soup. "If they says he's no king, then why give the man a king's death. If tis a common man, then use the execution of a common villain."

But I was here only to befriend Agnes Oats all over again. This school, having lost most of its funds once the war was declared over and the parliamentary forces the victors, now had only eight faithful pupils and no sons of wealthy aristocrats would choose to learn where the headmaster was a Puritan following only the doctrines of Oliver Cromwell.

With her nephew studying there, his dues first halved and the rest paid from her wages, Agnes joined the staff as matron, and had cooked both the roast pork and the cabbage broth, and was now shouting from the kitchens.

"I'll not nurse these brats and feed them three times a day, and wash the bloody platters too. You get that other wench in here."

I dutifully plodded into the kitchen, filled the bucket at the well, didn't bother to heat the water, sat on the low stool in front of the bucket, and began to wash the dishes. Smiling up at Agnes was the only advantage. "Nice that we've met already. Maybe it's months since we met, but it's good to rediscover old friends."

"Was we friends?"

How encouraging. "I believed so. I brought food for your nephew. I shared my shelter with you when the winds blew up."

The Little Ice Age, we called it afterwards. The warmth of the medieval had blistered into the Tudor freeze, then the frost filled years of the Restoration. But those were amongst the thousand things I couldn't speak of.

Instead I became the lowest ranking servant at the school, and there were so few of us since the place was virtually penniless, being the lowest meant little. I was fed and given a bed – having once been in the older boy's dormitory, carried into the little attic which became the servants' quarters, gave security. Smelly, web hung, scuttling cockroaches and squashed under the rafters, this at least offered sleep, even comfort, but I received no wages. Probably Agnes taking the bed next to mine was the least of my delights.

Apart from Agnes, Henry Bloom and myself, there were two others working at the failing school, both teachers, one of Latin being Simon Braithwaite, and the other pretending to teach mathematics. That was Master William Prestwich, who thought himself a man of brilliance, wit, and handsome attractions. I didn't think him anything of the sort but he could be hard to get rid of.

The second night I was there, he climbed into bed with me. I was suddenly grateful to Agnes. She yelled herself red in the face. "You get away from that trollop," she roared. "I ain't gonna pass my night listening to you two grunting and bumping."

But I was already out of bed, petticoats flying and my face almost as red as Agnes's. "There'll be nothing of the sort," I said loudly. "William Prestwich, how dare you. Now get out before I call Henry Bloom."

"You want us both together?" the idiot sniggered. "A rollicking threesome, I'd reckon."

"He'd sit on you and squash you flat."

Then Agnes hit him over the head with the oil lamp. William lay flat on his face, nose bleeding profusely. He scrambled up, one hand to his nose, and limped away swearing under his breath. Agnes followed him, swinging the heavy metal oil lamp. And that was when I really managed to call her friend. I even hugged her. She liked that although I didn't.

And now it was Sunday rules and Sunday regulations, and those who did not go to the church every Sunday would be severely fined. Having a cold, sore toes or a backache was not an acceptable excuse Agnes and I went to church together that Sunday, young Thomas between us. The church had been altered, although once a bright place of painted walls and a marble pulpit, it was plain now and lacked any ornament. The pulpit had been crushed and removed. A small wooden table stood there instead.

I had followed the law of modesty and was dressed in black and white, my head covered and as little of my body showing as was possible. Since I wasn't as poor as I pretended to be, I managed a reasonable costume. In spite of this, the preacher standing at his small wooden table, pointed a long white finger.

"That woman," he said, both voice and finger quivering, "is not suitably clothed."

I would have loved to argue, but that was hardly the best moment. We were told there would be no singing, no festivities, no feasts nor celebrations, no dancing, and, of course, no frills nor decorations, no satins nor velvets, no gold or silver and nothing whatsoever in the way of lipstick, face paint or hair curling.

I longed to ask what sort of god the preacher believed in, who was so mean-hearted, who had created us with love, but now withheld that love unless we gave up all avenues to happiness and entertainment. Why would a great and loving God care so bitterly about such trivial details? But of course, I sat meekly and gazed at my lap.

The morning had, however, inspired Agnes, and it seemed she had slightly changed. "What's that word?" she said as we trotted back to school and took off our cloaks. "Inspiration. That be the one. And that's what I got. Inspired." She smirked. "Now I knows my God and reckon if I loves him, he'll be loving me."

I nodded, since her opinion mattered not one jot, But I murmured, "Henry Bloom will approve of that."

"We must do as our Lord God wishes," she said, sounding smugly prim.

I left her to it. There were other matters to consider, especially since the wretched William, firmly believing that he was god's gift to women, was playing up again. Having waited one night until I was deeply asleep, he managed to climb into my bed without waking me. Agnes didn't wake either, or at least, not until I yelled. William already had one hand inside my petticoats and grabbing at my thighs. I kicked as hard as I could, bare foot, and he toppled from the bed. I told him loudly that if he ever did this again, I would report him to Henry Bloom, the local preacher, the myriad of printed brochures, the local sheriff and Oliver Cromwell himself if I could find him. I nearly added the police and the daily newspaper but luckily stopped myself since neither of these things yet existed.

When young Tom told me that the vile teacher had also stuffed his hand inside the boy's britches more than once, I was disgusted, hit the man over the head with the frying pan and told Agnes, expecting her to be furious. She didn't appear to care and I later discovered why. But a week later, William climbed into bed beside Agnes and that created chaos. Both hands were squeezing her breasts when she woke with a jolt, and while she was screaming blue murder, she punched William so viciously in the face that his nose didn't just bleed this time, it broke.

Frightened or simply ashamed, I didn't know or care. But the following day William left the school, and we were all excessively glad to see him gone.

"Creepy idiot," Agnes spat and that was true.

William had not simply been a handsome playboy, he had the ardent desire to be a rapist of anyone and everyone including men, women and children of both sexes. At first seemingly just an arrogant idiot, I soon started finding him both repulsive and criminal. It was after he'd left that I heard he had at some time buggered every single one of the children, had forced them to blow him off, and had insisted on watching them piss and then making them hold onto him while he pissed – a perverse idea that made me quite sick.

So without the vile behaviour of Master Prestwich, school life continued and gradually Henry Bloom, having made the announcement during one church service, attracted the sons of the local Puritan middle classes, and the failing school succeeded once more.

I offered to teach basic reading, writing and even some

extremely childish science. Rather surprised at being offered the services of a female who actually knew something worth teaching, Henry Bloom accepted and although two boys were taken off the school premises for this improper practise, I was able to continue, and in some quarters where the boy's parents approved. They would have approved even more had they known that William Prestwich's absence had saved their sons. The science became a quandary since I had to discover what was already known at that time, and so avoid teaching the modern bits and pieces I knew but which remained still unknown in the 1640s. However, teaching reading and writing was actually quite enjoyable, and I used modern methods, although lacking the computers of course, and had all those children reading in weeks. The parents I spoke to were astounded and either thought their son to be a genius, or decided that it was me. I just smiled.

The patient Simon Braithwaite took on mathematics alongside teaching Latin, and Henry Bloom added the Puritan scriptures to his efforts. Amazingly, I was out of the kitchen and was soon treated with vague respect. Agnes, sniffing at me when told to do the washing, remained as a servant, and two other maids were employed as we became more profitable.

Surprisingly comfortable now, I continued my work for some time, even collecting a small salary. But I was not improving my friendship with Agnes.

The bitter weather continued, and our high roofed rooms were chilly and doomed by draughts. When the puddles outside turned to ice, I could hear the threatening crack as of something malicious below the surface. It was worse whenever anyone walked over, and then sometimes the crack was less subtle, and the foolish stumbler splashed and swore as his boots filled with freezing water. But the little muffled cracks of threat were heard from under the ice, even when no one was near.

It made me think of demons.

CHAPTER FIFTEEN

I could neither enter Vespasian's mind as I did Sarah's (Oh, how I wish I could) nor might I be present during pre-trial discussions, but Vespasian later related what he found both amusing, and absurd.

He had spoken at length with Cromwell. As now a close member of Cromwell's associates, friends, supporters and political advisors, Vespasian, particularly in company, spoke as he wished.

"I had no expectation nor any specific desire to alter history," he told me, "but at that specific time I do not know how close our relationship needed to be. And a complacent supporter who might only say 'yes' to Cromwell's beliefs, was not what the fool wished for. Yet his temper can be an irritation."

And it seems that most of the people, even those who gladly supported him, were deeply concerned by the prospect of murdering an anointed king. One, nominated as the official judge, suddenly disappeared. Others refused to sign the accusation. Some walked out.

Fists clenched and eyes inflamed, Cromwell had roared about justice. "If this Charles had even the slightest shadow of a brain or the instincts of a rightful king, he would have followed his son abroad."

"Then you'd have called him a coward," Vespasian had interrupted.

'You will sign," Cromwell's voice raised even more and his lips narrowed. One fist clutched at his hair, and Vespasian saw the demon's eyes alight within the furious face. "It is the Lord God who empowers me, and only I know His will and judgement. This Charles called king must die. Or there will be uprisings in his name, rebellions, foreign invasions and calls for his return to power. I will not have such nonsense. My word would become challenged and even eroded. I will not have it, I tell you. This man must die."

"But, my Lord Cromwell," another said, "you speak of the crowned king of England, a monarch appointed by the Lord God himself."

"A charade," Cromwell had roared. "A falsity. Only I know the mind of our Lord and will impose it on the God-forsaken fools, demons and witches of this land."

The death warrant was finally signed by some, and Cromwell's signature came first. Many others carefully disappeared from the chamber when the time came, others simply refused. Cromwell preached justice, honesty and simple obedience to the scriptures, but ignored the holy anointing of the royal heir before the pulpit in God's name. Others were disturbed by the accusation of treason.

His majesty's trial was a farce, and even though I knew my history, now living here and surrounded by the opinions of a thousand others around me, I was horrified at the absurdity and disgraceful lack of justice. Charles was accused of treason. Since he was the king, very few people of England could understand how he could be treasonous against himself.

"Treason against his own people," seethed Cromwell between his teeth.

The parliament refused the undertaking at first, even the commons and then the lords balked at the idea. Finally, Cromwell forced the proceedings. His majesty was quickly tried for treason.

Having refused to answer any question, or even to defend himself, Charles explained that since the court had no power to accuse nor try him, he would neither speak nor afford the judge the honour of answering him.

In fact, the absurd attack of treason was made because this accusation did not involve calling a jury. A jury would never have brought in a guilty verdict. But the trial of anyone for treason demanded only the judgement of the court and judge themselves and absolved anyone who might find the accused king innocent.

The trial was therefore utterly ridiculous and his majesty sat completely silent during those first days, nor would he plead since the charge, he insisted, could not be legally put against him. He even managed to appear unmoved.

As the mock trial progressed, Charles spoke and remained both eloquent and convincing, but whatever he said now made not one snap of difference, for the judge had received his orders from Cromwell, and was already decided on his judgement.

It was during this time that finally I saw Vespasian again. Dressed as a Puritan without conviction, plain dark cloth but with cuffs turned back in velvet and a cravat of white linen, lace trimmed, he barely hid his religious doubts. I, however, was as insignificant as possible. So we did not stand together when he escorted me to the site of the proposed execution of our crowned and, some shouted, divinely chosen King Charles I.

"Alright," I muttered when I managed to stand at Vespasian's side, "how do they get away with it?"

The crowd was shuffling, some shouting, some crying. These were the common people who supported Cromwell, but the murder of their king was no popular act after all.

"Charles was – is – unfortunate," Vespasian told me without bothering to lower his already quiet voice. He was even harder to hear over the mutterings around us. "Like Henry VIII, Charles was a second son and was not educated to be king. When the elder brother died, Henry VIII took this as God's indication that he was the better man. Charles did not feel this way. He is desperately shy, and although a sweet and kindly man in private, he cannot relate to his subjects in public. His religious beliefs are profound and fervent, but in contrast to those of Cromwell. "

"So," I said, just as if I was back at school, "Charles and Cromwell are exact opposites."

"And yet so alike," Vespasian answered. "Both hold their religion as the ultimate guidance. Charles believes that God has placed him in a position of immense responsibility and therefore his life must consist of his duty to his people doing exactly whatever he believes is God's will. Cromwell follows a different God, one who demands the duty of austerity and orders Cromwell to lead the country into righteousness as he sees it. They are the same man. It is the church which varies."

"The same fanaticism," I mumbled, nodding, "the same arrogance and the same conviction that they alone know the right way. But Cromwell doesn't share the little king's sweet nature beneath the all-knowing arrogance, and doesn't love his people as Charles does."

Already he was walking away and I stood squashed within the crowd and watched as King Charles was brought out and led to the execution block. It was surrounded in black cloth, and here, at Whitehall in front of the banqueting hall, the day was freezing, being 30th January 1649 during England's little ice age when winter meant skating on the frozen rivers across all the country, including the Thames, while the very poor were dying in their unheated cottages.

I knew from books I'd read that Charles wore two warm shirts as he didn't want to shiver so much that the crowd would think him trembling with fear. I thought this dreadfully sad, but I could see little of the action, and no blink of the royal's face. I was too far back in the crowd, but I saw more than I ever wanted to remember afterwards. He knelt, bent his head to the block, stretched out his arms, and the executioner swung his axe. The stroke was clean and sudden and extremely quick. I turned away as the king's head was raised and shown to the crowd.

I heard cheering and clapping from some at the front. But from those around me there was a mighty gasp, followed by silence, and then by crying. The king's habits may not have been popular amongst many of his people, but he had still been the Lord's king. A king was a king was a king.

A pubic execution, I muttered to myself, was an aberration and a denial of humanity, whoever the dead might be. Even the worst criminal should have his privacy in which to die. This was a Roman massacre in the Colosseum – making pain and bloodshed into comic theatre.

I'd lost Vespasian and stumbled away alone. It was Agnes I bumped into.

"Well, 'tis done." She seemed content.

"Few of the people approved," I added. I realised I was crying too. After knowing of this death taking place 400 years ago, seeing the actual procedure felt worse than I'd expected. I couldn't stop crying.

My thoughts calmed and I called myself a fool. Centuries before I had seen mass slaughter and thought it right. Now I felt more like Sarah, disgusted at the open and bloody death of a simple and innocent man.

Then Agnes spat in my face. "And you a righteous follower? Or is you a king's whore after all, stupid bitch."

I wiped her disgusting spit from my cheek. "I'm not the only one crying. Half the crowd seems appalled," I said, turned away and walked off. How I was supposed to be her friend, I had no idea, but it was the only reason I was stuck at this school pretending to be a Puritan. I had always disliked Agnes since our first meeting. Now I loathed her. She was a bitch. Yet although she approved of bloodshed, all I had seen her do was mistreat her nephew and talk rubbish.

I walked home alone, trotted up to the attic dormitory, climbed fully dressed onto my bed, wiped my eyes and tried to think. Back to work, forget the king's execution, attempt to follow the teachings of the new church, make no complaints, and wait for Vespasian to reappear.

The children of titled royalists gradually faded from our dormitories, but we retained a good many boys between the ages of eight and twelve, including Tom who was now permitted a free education because of Agnes's presence, and since her wages were virtually a blink and a handshake, even the half fees Tom had once had to pay, were now dissolved. I slouched, slept, woke, ate meagre nothings and spent my days teaching the simple basics of reading and writing. My own problems writing with a quill pen, slopping ink and blotting paper was my only difficulty, and something which some of the boys managed better than I did.

Sleeping was no problem since I was tired enough each day to close my eyes at night and blink immediately into dreams. But the dreams, over which I had no control, were nightmares of eyes amongst the trees, shifting shapes howling and the malicious threats which haunted me day and night. I had escaped my own garden. Yet it had followed me.

Shadows, ice, the whine of the wind and the tumultuous rain all made me shiver. But there was also bird song, the patter of badger paws, the big golden eyes of the hungry fox and the sudden sighting of a deer between the far trees. And so I concentrated on the sweet and the beautiful, yet could not ignore the doomed pulse of the ugly and the threatening.

Worse came. The well had clogged up. Not an unusual problem at that time. Water was frozen, or at least so frosted that it could not flow even underground. Dead birds fell into the pits, even dead foxes and rats. Sometimes it was just the pump that had frozen.

It certainly wasn't my job to discover the reason nor try to clear the blockage, but Agnes had been sent to fill a bucket, and said a straight no, since it was impossible. "Dig another damned well," she said. Having shocked Henry Bloom with her language, she stalked off and he went to find Simon.

Simon found me. "I'll not ask you to dig, mistress," he muttered, somewhat insulted at having been ordered to do such a job. "But I'd be much obliged if you'd stand by me to hold the bucket and such."

I agreed. Simon was no hulking great brute and I thought he was a bit of a weakling. So was I, as it happened, but two weaklings can make one strong man.

He bent over the edge of the well's lip, hanging onto the pump so as not to fall, and peered down into the deep shadows. I asked him if he could see anything. He said he could see a blockage, although not clearly, so didn't know what it was. "I'll help you haul it out," I offered as he rolled over, clutching his nose. As he staggered up, he was gagging.

"A stink down there," he pointed. "Reckon 'tis a dead dog."

I had already smelled the putrid stench. Holding my breath, I shoved down the long narrow spade and dug up a bulge of wet muck, tipping it out on the side of the pump. I looked but not too closely. "It's a dead something," I agreed. And it was about the size of a stray dog. I certainly felt the sympathy, but the smell was too strong to get closer.

"That all?" Simon asked.

So I shoved the spade down again and managed to drag up a few more small clumps of gunge. "It's got a bit solid," I explained, "or too big. I need a pitchfork or a rake if I'm to bring out anymore."

"Well, we needs to clear it," muttered Simon, "nor we ain't got no water, nor clean nor dirty," and he stomped off to find a rake.

I stood there, waiting, and gazing with extreme distaste at the dead dog. The whole stench seemed to be getting stronger now some of the thing was up in fresh air, rising almost like a cloud or a mist around the pile I'd unearthed, and I took another step away. And then I saw the finger.

From the mulch, the top of a finger, its nail black and the skin below lined in decay. So amazed that I didn't even retch, I stared and then from a distance, poked the pile with my spade. Bits fell separate. There was a cloth, a sheet perhaps, though so filthy it was difficult to recognise. It was easier to recognise what had been wrapped within. There was a hand, then another hand. One tumbled, bones cracked, from a long naked arm.

That was when I was sick, gagging until my throat was raw and my eyes streaming.

Simon came back carrying the long-handled rake and stared to where I was pointing. With a grunt of horror, he hurried to the well and thrust in the rake. Within moments he had hooked up a pile of the stinking mush, and immediately tried again. It was sometime before he was sure to have hoisted it all, and left the well running free. Not clean, perhaps. But human remains now lay scattered on the mud and frost around us.

This seemed even worse than my dreams, perhaps my dreams becoming truth. I had vomited almost continuously until nothing was left to bring back. So reluctantly, and holding my stomach as if it might fall out, I walked back to the muck from the well. It was badly decayed, and much was still indistinguishable from simple slime and jelly, but the rest was obvious enough.

Now having completed his task, Simon had marched in the opposite direction and was filling another bush with his vomit. I was left alone to study the stuff spread at my feet. One human arm still supporting a hand, was unattached to a body, but the torso, naked, lay on its back with half an arm attached on one side. Another hand was knotted into a fist but lay alone. The lower half of the body was mutilated, the stomach gaping open and the pelvis sliced down the middle. The body was clearly masculine, and a small part of the genitals remained. Three chopped off fingers clutched at those miserable remains.

His legs and two feet lay in several hacked pieces. Where the body parts had been bundled together, they remained decayed but visible. Other parts were just smashed bone, lumps of sodden flesh, and scraps of hair.

There was no head, no face, however unrecognisable, and no clear sign of what had happened.

When Simon crawled back, he was as miserable as I was. "Someone fell down this damned well," he said, swearing for the first time since I'd known him, "and couldn't climb out, poor fellow. He died here, screaming for help but was never heard."

"Then where's his clothes?" I demanded.

"Obvious, ain't it?" Simon said, shaking his head. "Naked in bed. Came out for fresh air, or some bad dream. Fell in the hole without seeing it."

"Then," I asked softly, "where's his head?"

"Stuck further down," Simon suggested with a gulp. "Fell headfirst."

I said that didn't make sense. "You mean he drowned, his head under water, and when the neck rotted through, the head's weight took it down to the bottom of the well." I suppose it might be possible although I doubted it. "But with his hand around his mutilated bits?" I continued, unable to say the word. "And the sheet?"

"He were naked so wrapped the sheet around hisself like a cloak. Simple."

"I think I recognise those hands." Both were blackened and partly decayed but the thick fingered and wide palmed hands, one hanging on a narrow wrist too small seemingly for the solid and stumpy hand it supported, were what I had seen and disliked many times. "I know who it is."

Shaking his head, Simon gagged again. "It ain't him. Not a good man maybe, but no man deserves a wicked death like this."

So he recognised it too. "This is William Prestwich," I said softly, "and he's been murdered."

Staring, Simon's mouth dropped open. "No way, mistress, murder? Not possible."

I had very little forensic knowledge, but I'd watched relevant programmes on TV. I said, "It's two weeks since William disappeared. I think this sort of decay is about right for that. What was it? Twelve days, that's right. But having no head just isn't possible unless someone cut his throat. The whole neck couldn't have decayed away faster than any other part. And the legs have been chopped up. That's not natural disintegration. The belly all ragged. And the bits in his hand – that's a straight cut. And where's his ring? He always wore that thin little silver band, didn't he. He said it was a gift from his mother."

Discarding both rake and spade, Simon turned and raced back to the kitchens within the school, yelling about what we'd found. Agnes glared and yelled back that this was nonsense. The other two maids, eyes glazed and cheeks white, came rushing to hear what the noise was all about, and Henry Bloom marched in to complain. The children, forbidden to enter the kitchen at all times, clustered outside the doorway, fascinated by the chaos.

"Murder," screeched Simon.

"Absolute rubbish," growled Henry.

"No, it isn't," I said, coming up behind. "It's the truth. We did our best to unblock the well, but it can't be used again Not now. We found the dead and mangled body parts of a man. I'm fairly sure it's William Prestwich."

One maid fainted into Henry's arms and the other became hysterical, screaming at me without words.

I looked at Agnes. She glared at me, but there was a slight twist to her mouth, and a dimple at each corner. That was when I realised that she'd done it. This woman who had lately adopted a more deeply Puritan religion, had slaughtered a man in cold blood. A disgusting man of course, but only a disgusting woman could kill and mutilate, chopping into the legs and amputating the entire head. Then to sling the parts down the well, which might have poisoned our water supply. And, remembering a recent gown bought new, I guessed she'd stolen and then sold that silver ring.

I had no proof against her, but I wasn't surprised. She fostered a demon, and this was the first time I'd really seen its work.

I approached her that evening in our tiny dark dormitory. The two maids hadn't come upstairs yet, since the doctor had been called. Agnes sat on her own bed and looked back at me. "You knows, don't you?" she said with that little twisted smile. I nodded.

"Did you catch that pig hurting Tom?" That seemed the most likely motive. "Or did he try and rape you again?"

She didn't bother explaining. "Reckon I'll tell yer one day," she said. "But first you gotta swear never to tell no one. When the sheriff gets called, and there'll be all sorts o' regulators and churchy fellows surging all around reckoning they ought to know who to blame afore the school gets closed down. And there ain't no one 'cept you what knows it were me."

"I won't tell." This was surely going to be my own opportunity to catch the demon and do what I had seen Vespasian do in our garden. He said he would do it again with my help, but he hadn't told me not to try. I wanted to see what I might manage.

CHAPTER SIXTEEN

Cromwell pronounced himself Lord Protector and might as well have called himself king. In a way, he was. But there was unrest in every part of the country not only amongst those who were appalled at the murder of the rightful king, whether they had thought him a good king or not, but also amongst those who wanted Cromwell to alter his ideas and intentions.

I was still hobbling around and avoiding Agnes as the sheriff and his men came to investigate. More than half the pupils were quickly taken from the school by their horrified parents, and once again the place withered, fell bankrupt and left everyone miserable. Except Agnes.

The victim of her malice hadn't even been one of the figures carrying a demon, even though he had been utterly vile, and I bet a dozen demons had been having a party inside the wretched man.

Now life was changing in other ways. No singing and no dancing, no feasting and no colour, no joy and no love. A couple of little boys playing football were snatched up and whipped. A woman wearing make-up was grabbed in the street and her face scrubbed. Those working on a Sunday would be fined and anything which suggested happiness was banned. Work hard for six days, and rest on Sunday after church. Otherwise, said the new doctrine, you'll never get to heaven. Christmas frivolity was banned. No decorations, no feasts and no music. Church first and then prayer, concentrating only on the birth of the Lord.

"Follow my example," Cromwell told us. "And heaven will wait for you." I muttered under my breath as did everyone around me.

"He's almost thinking he's God. He thinks he's the guardian of heaven." I had been the Gate Keeper myself, although not of heaven of course. But I didn't want to think about that anymore.

Pointless enjoyment? No – that was wicked. Swearing more than one stutter meant imprisonment. Strict fasting on Saint's days was obligatory. A pleasant walk in the countryside on a Sunday? Never! Or accept a large fine – perhaps even sit in the stocks for a day.

In towns and larger villages there always sat the stocks, those wooden prisons where those condemned for punishment were dragged, their legs and sometimes their arms trapped and locked there for one day, two days, or even three. Surrounded by the stones, rotten vegetables and dirty water, even piss, thrown by the righteous, they were brought ale to drink but rarely food. Folk laughed as they passed, ignoring the lowered face of the miserable prisoner who had perhaps sworn at the neighbour who kicked his dog, or sung to his wife on a Sunday. If the prisoner rebelled against his punishment and jeered those who threw their rubbish at him, he might be whipped before being set free.

Avoiding the town square or the village green where the stocks usually stood prominent, I hated these public displays of punishment. These were not Cromwell's invention, but he encouraged their use for such minor crimes including those behaviours which were obviously not crimes at all. But the damned man was a hypocrite and was reported indulging a few of the diversions he banned for others.

With a deep hatred for the elaborations of the Catholic church, Cromwell failed to understand hatred as being the first thing that ought to be banned. I'd never even met the man, but I disliked him intensely from what I'd heard. I'd never met the king either, and thought him a man of horribly rigid ideals and a poor leader, but a far nicer person and a loving family man who tried so hard to do his best in spite of his lack of confidence and bitter shyness.

And then the massacre. Although Cromwell now governed the country, the Irish remained faithful to Catholicism. Cromwell was furious. When rebellion arose, he ordered the massacre of both rebels and citizens, adults and children, both fighters and those who had surrendered. The massacre was horribly brutal, and Cromwell's forces were encouraged to be violent. Those children not murdered were collected and sent abroad as slaves. Cromwell's demon had reached its peak. It was a little later that Vespasian told me his story.

The Lord Protector had returned to England extremely tired but entirely exultant. He had rid the world of enough Catholics to prove his good intentions to his god.

Although I doubted he was motivated by more than the wish for freedom, Vespasian had never accepted any position on the parliament benches nor as a soldier in the new army. He had no intention of fighting under Cromwell's orders, and remained simply an occasional friend and advisor.

It was as advisor that Vespasian sat opposite at the table, their pottage bowls empty and pushed aside, a pile of papers in their place. Vespasian, leaning back, had remarked, "So, my friend, you feel that the exercise in Ireland was successful?"

"Do you doubt it?" Cromwell looked up, frowning. "I have

completed one of my greatest services to the Lord and His holy church."

Vespasian, cold eyed, might often stay silent but never spoke an outright lie. "I cannot agree," he said. "These people are your people. They believe in the same God even though they worship in another fashion. All humanity learns at its own pace."

Pushing his chair back, Cromwell stood and watched as the entire table tipped and his papers were flung across the toppling chairs and the floorboards beneath. "You want me furious? I thought you my friend."

"Which is why," Vespasian continued, "I have the courage to question your beliefs. You are free, naturally, to convince me of your righteousness."

"I should not need to convince you," Cromwell said, pulling back another chair as Vespasian rose and set the table back on its feet. He did not bother to collect the scattered papers.

"I know your idealism," he said. "But never have I known you to massacre those who have not raised arms against you, including their children. I believe this harsh. I believe it unchristian."

Scowling, "And I believe it God's will. Our Lord has preached against idolatry and wicked practises. The children I ordered killed, and those sent abroad, would have grown up Catholic. What I do, and what I order, is all for the Lord God. It is never for myself."

"And I've heard you claim that the Lord resides in your heart?"

"He does." Almost whispering, "Sometimes I feel His presence, and it is overpowering." Cromwell calmed, leaned down and began to grab at the papers littering the floor.

As he bent so Vespasian rose, and walked forwards as if to help. But instead he forced both hands around the other man's forehead and very softly said the words, "Somnum penitus."

Alarmed and briefly indignant, Cromwell struggled, but then fell, surrendering abruptly, his eyes closed. Vespasian pressed, spreading his fingers and cupping his palms, enclosing Cromwell's brow and head within his own power.

Waiting just a heartbeat for the demon's distress to swell, Vespasian knelt beside him, opened Cromwell's eyelids with one finger and replaced his hands around the other's skull as before. He sat then, staring into the newly opened eyes, now stark green, as emerald as the jewel newly polished.

"You have proved yourself strong," Vespasian said very softly.

The reply was a screech, half high pitched and then guttural. "I can do better," said the voice, cackling without breath. "I have plans. I'm no fool, human, and I know my limitless capacity. Within me are twelve other demons I've used to create myself invincible. With twelve inside, already eaten, and this human sucked almost dry, I am a great and wondrous icon. How many have you within you, human? I'll swear you cannot outnumber me."

Digging the balls of his thumbs deeper into Cromwell's temples, Vespasian smiled. "I do not wish to eat the strength of others," he said. "I am alight with the power of my own magic, and I command you to come forward and prove yourself to me beyond the compass of the human where you hide."

Cromwell's body rolled, heaving, as though the thing inside clung tightly against the command to reveal itself.

Vespasian repeated the order. "Come out, or I shall call on Lilith to reclaim you. Show yourself and prove yourself."

The green eyes swirled outwards, bulging and then glazed. For a moment they seemed to float above the man's head, his own eyes closed once more. The crackling voice said, "If I come, I will kill you, human. Do not tempt me."

"Tempt you?" Vespasian laughed. "I call you. I invite. I release you from your human decanter. I demand you. Come out and dare to show yourself."

The voice diminished. "I am warm here. Why should I face you? I would enter you if I wished and take you over as I have this creature's bulk and vision. This human sack is obedient to me and thinks me righteous and calls me his lord. I have no need for another."

With his fingers stretching downwards, Vespasian forced open the mouth, its lips previously clamped, and abruptly breathed hot and fast into the throat. The demon gulped and fire flew from the eyes. Cromwell's body squirmed.

A slow rattle, sounding like the self-protection of the rattlesnake, gargled from Cromwell's mouth, and the stench of something rotten increased. Then fragments of moving black shadow squelched outwards, covering the green eyes and swallowing the light of the candles in the room.

A black fog drifted high, surrounding both Cromwell and Vespasian. It thickened and started to swirl, misting deeper like the smoke from a burning pit. Vespasian coughed, but breathed again into the throat he held open. Again, the smoke intensified, thick black, swirling quicker and plunging down towards Vespasian's head. He permitted it to gather until it blinded him, biting into his face. Then he blew faster and harder.

The black swathes of grit and filth rushed at him, but could not enter his mouth. It gathered, pushing at him and glowing with both soot and flame. Now the mist was no longer black and burst open with spiralling threads of furnace.

Again, it clustered, buzzing now like a wasp's nest, but unable to enter Vespasian's mouth. He continued to blow. But he no longer blew into Cromwell's mouth, but directly at the cloud.

Gathering force, the cloud condensed further becoming a fat thick ball of darting eyes, red as coals, with tears like raging floods of blood from each eye socket, and pupils turning from scarlet to pitch.

And still Vespasian blew. He was muttering words, repeating over and over, and the words took shape in his own throat although his mouth was open and his breath a billowing force into the bluster beyond.

Quite suddenly with a wail of utter failure, the cloud began to disintegrate. Its compaction gradually opened. Shreds rolled off and out like pasta cooking in boiling water. The smoke drifted, and the eyes closed. Their bleeding tears simmered and dissolved. The cloud became a mist once again. It had thinned and wisps sprang away as Vespasian continued to blow.

The wisps became fragmented arms and circled both above his head and around him, seething and spitting black dust. The fragments twisted, becoming a hundred fingers, yet not one was able to grasp Vespasian's body, and he now blew at any darkness around him, as though finally clearing a fire. He did not stop and the last trails of darkness fell to the ground as if too tired to continue the battle.

Vespasian stopped blowing. He stamped on the grains of rotting ash beneath his feet, ground them into dust and then held both hands over the last grains, as tiny as grass seed. He picked those two grains up between his fingers and spoke quietly.

"You must now be gone. You are no longer either demon or cruelty. You are the forgotten memory of Lilith's symbolism and you cannot rise again. In the name of Zeamandrax, I banish you to the sanctuary of forgetfulness. You are no more."

The smear on his palm disappeared entirely. His palm was clean. Vespasian turned and gazed down at Cromwell. Then he bent, and slowly helped him up.

Cromwell blinked, and leaning on Vespasian's arm, levered himself onto the chair. He sat heavily, rubbing his eyes. Some of the papers were still tight in his hand. He blinked at Vespasian, who remained at his side, his hands beneath his arms.

"Thank you, friend," Cromwell stuttered. "How did I fall?"

"A dizzy moment, nothing more," Vespasian had said, which means he did sometimes lie after all. "But if you feel well enough, I must leave and return to my own duties. Shall I call your wife?"

"No." Cromwell stood, and shook his head with a wide and unexpected smile. "No need to worry her," he said. "Indeed, I feel surprisingly well. Better than for many months. The fighting, you know, the Irish, the king. All to be forgotten now. I am myself again."

"Indeed you are," said Vespasian softly, moving towards the door. "And I trust will remain so for those years remaining."

Cromwell called after him, "A strange experience, and I have no explanation. Yet, perhaps, although it was you, my friend, who helped me up, I believe it was my Lord who spoke to me as I stumbled. No doubt it was not simply a dizzy moment, but a true call of the Holy Word. God visits me indeed, friend Jasper. You have been present during a heavenly moment, and that is also a blessing on you. Such moments are rare for most. Even I do not experience them often." Shaking his head as though clearing some wisp of confusion he added, "Now no voice whispers to me, nor comforts me. But I know He will return for I am His son and ardent disciple. I accept that His words are rare."

Vespasian, as he told me afterwards, had paused for just one smile, saying, "Some such experiences, Master Cromwell, need to be very rare indeed."

CHAPTER SEVENTEEN

And that's what Vespasian told me later. Delighted and fascinated, I begged him to repeat so many details, I think he got bored.

"My dearly beloved," he said, half grinning with a touch of exaggerated irony, "this is indeed what we came to do, and it was never expected to be a sudden or fast success. Yet now, even one less of the devil's creatures invading our own home will be a vast benefit. If we can annihilate the second and third, we can return to Randle in peace."

"There are others with demons," I insisted. "I've met some. One vile man is dead, and I know Agnes killed him, but he was a demon himself."

"No matter," Vespasian said, walking across to our small mullioned window. "All those fragments set free by Lilith's temporary destruction will congregate and suffer the absorption by those stronger. Destroying the origin of the most powerful, automatically destroys all those later taken by one which no longer exists."

We were back in our cottage, snug and cosy, and very considerably benefiting from some small advantages which

Vespasian had brought with us from our modern home, hot water, for instance, and warmth even when the frost outside turned to ice. And I felt warmer still, for now I had heard another description of how to destroy a demon.

"Time," I said, "is a very mysterious business. I used to think it always travelled in a straight line."

"There are no straight lines in nature," Vespasian said, his back to me.

"But," I muttered, "All I am doing, while you do the miracles, is teaching kids to read and plodding around trying to look pure. I can't even make custard."

Turning, Vespasian looked down and smiled, brushing my hair back from my eyes. "You want to prove your strength, as Cromwell does? But we are neither of us here by choice. We have come here because of circumstances, which is how all life throws itself at us, teaching us to read just as you teach your pupils."

"Teaches us?" I objected. "You once told me everything is symbolic." I felt like grumbling. What I really wanted to do was dance, and sing, and decorate Christmas trees, and make love with Vespasian on the grass. Most of all I wanted to prove I could kill demons and not just stir custard.

"Every house and home is symbolic of the family who lives within it. If your home is small, then you have concentrated only on certain aspects of your spiritual growth. If your home lacks personality, then either you have none, or you wish to avoid facing the personality hiding within. If you are homeless, then you have possibly failed to face your own problems, and if your home is beautiful and cosy, then you are facing your growth and working towards self-understanding. There are a million more patterns of essence symbolized by the shadows in which we live. Our home is symbolic of us, my love, and therefore easy for all beings from both worlds to trace those who, they think, set them free."

"Oh, Vespasian dearest," I sighed. "I'm tired of learning. Must I learn more?"

He bent over and very lightly kissed my forehead. "The physical life we recognize is entirely symbolic of who we are, and the world beyond our physical death. That, spiritual and not physical, is the reality." This time he kissed the tip of my nose. "Enough, my beloved. We have work to do." And he walked back to the window. "Out there," he continued, "are the suffering victims of the demon-fed. At least some, we can help and others can be freed."

"So we all think our solid touchable world is the real one, and the mystical is the symbol. But actually, you're saying it's the other way around." I added, leaning back in my dull Puritan gown, complete with white linen apron. "I suppose that means I'm pathetic as a symbol and equally pathetic underneath. Were all women supposed to feel like servants?"

"Another age of discrimination."

"And you already know the next problem, don't you?" He looked up, nodding. "It's Sarah Harrington, she's disappeared."

After many attempts to slip back into her mind, I had become extremely worried. I couldn't sense her, neither awake nor asleep, and the easy avenue of her identity was now closed against me and even locked. I had started to think she might be dead.

He paused, closing his eyes briefly, as though searching. Finally, "No, not dead," Vespasian crossed back to me, looking down into my eyes. I loved that look, showing the tunnels winding deeply back from eyes to thought. "I believe you will find her," he said, "if you continue to delve into your own past."

Well, all right the poor girl was me, younger and powerless, with the demon-invaded husband she loathed. I had begun to really believe he had killed her.

Something was keeping me out of her thoughts, and if she

was still alive, then she must surely be somehow closed off to the world, her thoughts wild and impossible to understand. Or perhaps she was ill.

But three days later, I found her. She was crying. I hurried back into her mind, closing off my own thoughts so that I might become less of myself. As usual, I felt her consciousness. Now I was Sarah Harrington again, but there was a difference.

I can see only the wooden slats of the four walls surrounding me. They are dust covered with faint wafts of spiders' webs and the dirt of many years.

No – there are two more things that I see. I have a bed. It is narrow and dishevelled without eiderdown or pillows. I have a blanket, which is grubby with tears, and a

pillowcase stuffed with rags. Beneath the bed is a chamber pot.

There is nothing else, except the outline of a doorway. No handle of course and locked from the outside. A tiny crack at the top of the door allowed a squeezed peep outside. Sadly, this did not help at all, for all I saw was leaves. Sometimes I said good morning to those leaves. But the crack also closed at night with the frost and the bitter draughts. I clutched my one blanket and pulled it over my head.

I kept track of the days by taking off one shoe and using the heel to scrape lines on one wall where the wood was damp and spongy. So I knew it had been eight days since Arthur threw me in here. The first day I sat shivering in complete terror and confusion. The next day I begged for food but when he laughed at me, I found the courage to jump up and scratch his face. Knocked back by both his fists, I collapsed with one black eye and a bleeding lip. The following day he brought me food but tied my left wrist to the bed so I couldn't escape past him, or attack him in return.

It took me four days to gnaw through the rope, and now it is a full day that I have sat here free, waiting for Arthur to bring me food and water so that I can escape and kill the son of a whore if I can.

He was sure I had poisoned him in order to take Jasper into my bed. Yet I also believed he had no such idea and had made it up so as to imprison me with good cause. Perhaps he swung from one to the other. Because there was another reason for what he had done, and he took advantage almost every evening.

My husband had never been interested in normal sexual coupling, and it is possible that he cannot truly achieve it. I didn't think I had to explain that. I simply meant that without his passions fired by cruelty, taking woman to bed didn't interest him in the least.

At first when married, I had no idea what coupling in the normal manner would be like and so I took Arthur's behaviour as the general expected behaviour and therefore what everybody did as a matter of course. I therefore thought that either I was a simpleton to dislike this so much, or that other women who pretended to enjoy the act, must be lunatic hussies.

About four or five months later I discovered the truth. My maid at that time, later told to leave as she had become almost motherly towards me having seen my bruises, explained a great deal. I told her where the injuries had originated, and she told me how wrong that was. At first her short pushing descriptions puzzled me, but after I had begged her, she described in more detail. "A husband," she murmured, not daring to speak loudly, "or indeed, any kind man who cares for you, first wants to experience your pleasure. Not his own. And then your pleasure actually becomes his delight."

I saw nothing more of Patty, but I managed to give her a gold necklace of mine before she went, told her to sell it at Cheapside and hoped it would keep her in some comfort for a year or so.

And now I knew that beating and pinching, biting, whipping

and cutting were not the normal passions of a normal man, at Arthur's insistence on swiving at my behind, and using large objects of intrusion first, were the actions of an unnatural and cruel man who loved to hurt, and not to please.

I had fallen in love with Cromwell's advisor, and that made me feel even more strongly the disgust I felt for the monstrous Arthur. Jasper Fairweather, although denying me his bed, had proved to me what touch might bring. Joy – instead of pain and misery.

So then, gradually summoning courage, I had started to refuse my husband. Once I ran. Meeting with the butler, I stopped to talk as long as I dared and Arthur slouched off to the library. On another occasion I had forced a pillow against him until he lost the capacity to swive at all and went limp.

So now I was here.

Not only could I not break free, I could not deny him while starving hungry and tied tight by one wrist. I also believe the captivity, and his ability to rape and perform disgusting deeds on a woman entirely under his power, and suffering for many reasons, could only bring delight to a demon. I so very much despised a man who could not find pleasure unless he tortured another. I wriggled my fingers.

Having that arm free at last from the bondage of the rope, was the beginning of the rest of my life. Courage again. I repeated the word over and over, as if the word itself would bring the deed.

At the beginning I had screamed of course. But this was a small and usually locked shed near the back of our grounds, and next to the pond where only the ducks could hear me. I begged more often than screaming and swearing, but that was just as futile. Now I had planned my escape – but not that of fleeing back to my house. I was going to get away to some distant place where I could not be traced. If I had the opportunity to murder the man, then I'd take it. But this seemed doubtful.

The pain was always horrific when it happened, but it was afterwards that it often seemed worse. Day after endless day sitting staring at the dust on the walls, or lying on the bed trying to think of the future and what happiness it might bring, was my only chance at forgetting the endless hours. Each little minute seemed like a lifetime. Each hour crept by so slowly that I thought I might go mad. Whatever pain had recently been inflicted on me, inevitably grew worse as time passed. The black eye felt as though my cheek had smashed, my split lip as if my chin was broken. Pain increased each night and then again in the morning. The back ache was probably caused by the lumpy bed and no possibility of exercise. I could walk three steps forwards, then three steps back. Neck ache from twisting and turning, gritting my teeth and cursing. Stomach ache like the stabbing of a knife caused by terrible hunger. A raw throat from lack of anything to drink and screaming. Then the cold, the shivering, the fear and the utter misery.

Hatred of my husband was equalled only by hatred of the god that had allowed this to happen. But then I feared God's revenge if I dared to hate him, and wondered if my support of the late king and dislike of Cromwell's intolerant beliefs was my crime, and Cromwell's god was already punishing me for that.

Planning my escape, I knew where I'd go, and being homeless didn't bother me. Already my clothes were that of some beggar maid. When Arthur had grabbed me, I was wearing two petticoats, a tight bodice but no skirt yet, and only one sleeve attached. I was sitting in front of the mirror in my bed chamber, half dressed and waiting for my maid to return with a cup of chocolate. I wore stockings and shoes but as yet no skirt and only one sleeve, so I had my bed robe over my shoulders like a shawl. This was all that had kept me warm ever since.

CHAPTER EIGHTEEN

My husband arrived shortly afterwards. I heard him clumping along the path and unlocking the door. He couldn't lock the door behind him since no lock existed on the inside, but he didn't yet know that I had freed my wrist.

Bending over me, Arthur grasped my ankle and flung me backwards. I tumbled back on the bed, legs flailing. The damned man hadn't even brought me food, let alone asked me how I was. Without a word he knelt between my legs and loosened the buttons on his britches. There was a willow cane stuck down his belt, and the belt itself was quickly unbuckled, ready for a beating.

I had thought of my escape, planned it for so long, now I had built up the courage to do it. So I immediately kicked both hard shoes into his groin, then his stomach, and even harder into his groin for the second time.

He looked amazed, finally he howled like a wolf, and toppled off me onto the floor, clutching his belly with one hand, the other trembling between his legs. I jumped up and stamped both feet onto his face. His cheek opened like a joint of meat, and bled with profusion. He groaned, gulped, shivered and clutched at every wounded part of him. I promptly stamped on his chest, and he gasped, then wheezed, unable to speak.

One last pleasure – I poured the contents of my chamber pot over his face, and then slipped off my shoes, held them, and ran.

I didn't have time to feel either guilty or proud, but I did know I was lucky. He had been too surprised to defend himself and it had all been quicker and easier than I had expected. Yes, I was lucky, and knew it. Perhaps the lack of retaliation was simply because my attack was so sudden and besides, he was a cowardly weakling behind all the bravado and cruelty. Maybe that was why he behaved in such a vile manner, boosting his inner knowledge of himself.

Not that I cared. I just ran.

My stockings were ruined of course, and my feet wet at once, but I could run faster without shoes, and getting far away was the most important goal of all.

It had rained several times in the past few days, so the fields were muddy and roads were puddled and pitted, but I hardly noticed and kept running until my breath gave out. There was no sign of Arthur following me, but he had possibilities which I did not. A good horse, for instance. Even a carriage, since he had his own small hackney, if he could get it fitted up in time.

Crawling up from the shed to the house would hopefully take him nearly an hour. I had time, so I climbed the little verge and the hedge beyond the lane and cut through the forested grasses and the fields beyond.

The first time I slept out in the cold, I was horrified. I hadn't realised it would be so cold and wet, and although I carpeted my muddy bed with dry leaves first, stripping the trees above me, the damp still seeped through and I had only my bed robe as a blanket. I could have grabbed the old blanket from the shed but had not thought of it. Too busy stamping and kicking! So much for planning.

That first night I could hardly sleep. In ignorance I had chosen to sleep beneath the shelter of the trees. Instead they dripped on me continuously. I stared out at the thousands of glowing stars like tiny torches showing me the way. No moon that first night, but the beauty of the stars glittering silver against the rich black sky was wonderful. It made me feel small, but it reminded me of the church preaching that God watched over us.

I slept perhaps an hour or a little more from utter exhaustion, then clambered up, shook out the muck from my clothes and continued my hopeful escape.

After the third night, I was accustomed to the wet freeze, but walked in almost constant mud, even when I walked only in my shoes. The only time the mud did not stick, was when it had frozen, making me slip. My hair was so woven with mud, it clung to my face. When at last there was a mild day, the mud baked, and I was able to pick some off.

Whether anyone had made the slightest effort to follow me and bring me home, I had not the smallest idea. I saw no one except children playing under an orchard of apple trees, and a woman collecting twigs for her fire. I had caught some form of mild ailment for I coughed and sneezed a great deal. Sleeping outside may have caused it. Yet it did not bother me too much, and I had energy enough to run, to climb, and to keep walking across the countryside. I began to sleep far better and even enjoyed the fresh frosty air in my throat. Instead of the usual smoke-filled gloom of most houses, I could enjoy the utter perfection of God's good country air. But I began to lose track of the days passing, and one morning I wondered if I had been walking only a few days, or perhaps a month. Not that it mattered. I was delighted to be away, free, and not having to comply with my husband's cruel demands.

Getting something to eat was harder. I ate nothing but apples for two days. I found mushrooms and old acorns, but could not cook them. Water, clean and cold, was easy from several narrow streams, and I also tried hard to wash myself. Then wet hair turned to icicles in the night and I coughed more. But carried on, even when so hungry I had lost my strength.

I couldn't count the days and lost track of time passing, but now, instead of each hour seeming like a day, each hour whizzed by like an arrow from a crossbow. My legs were hopelessly scratched, and I certainly felt the terrible cold when I tried to sleep. But running, climbing and walking kept me warm during the days and even the wistful sunshine tried to help.

When I saw the cottage standing all alone on the outskirts of a village, although not knowing where I was or what the village was called, I succumbed to the wrenching pain of hunger, and I knocked on the door to ask for bread, cheese if I was lucky again, or any tiny particle of food they could spare.

It was a pretty cottage, its thatched roof neat and well-trimmed, although glittering with tiny threads of ice. That was pretty too, as if decorated, remembering Christmas in the old days when we were permitted to hand mistletoe and holly and cook great feasts for our guests.

When the door abruptly opened, swinging back against the side of the house, just wattle and daub and so shook a little as though trembling with anticipation, one of those icicles dislodged and tipped directly onto my head. There the ice caught in the filthy knots, and I scrabbled to push my tangle of dirty curls from my eyes.

Then I felt a strong long fingered hand against my forehead, smoothing back the mud encrusted mess away from my face, eyes and ears, and then with one fingertip, someone wiped away the wet dirt from around my mouth.

I mumbled a thank you, sniffed in case my nose was dripping, rubbed my eyes so that I could see properly, and then realised the miracle. I'd prayed for more luck, but I would never have imagined I might deserve as much luck as this.

He stood there so calmly on the doorstep, tall and beautiful and smiled faintly, just a twitch at the corner of his mouth as I stared back at him, open mouthed. Then I snapped my mouth shut, and Jasper said, "You appear just a little lost, young lady."

I was. I was also standing there in front of this well dressed gentleman with his touches of non-Puritan velvet and lace, while I was wearing one bedraggled and torn sleeve and one bare arm, a torn petticoat which now seemed only to be filthy with the hems unravelling and wet, holes in my stockings and shoes thick with mud, mud caked hair in knotted tangles down to my shoulders, and my face striped like a tabby cat but with dirt. Clutched around me I wore what was clearly a bed-coat, which was also now mud encrusted. I coughed like a disease-ridden beggar brat, but even beggar brats didn't usually look quite as bad as me.

"No," I said. "But frozen and starving."

"In which case," he said very quietly, "you had best come in."

He held the door open for me and did not seem perturbed when I dripped my filth onto his rug. He closed the door gently behind me and asked me to sit while he fetched food. I then further ruined his room by sitting on his comfy chair, imprinting it no doubt with wet mud.

Jasper's little house was beautiful and seemed larger inside then out. Two small mullioned windows sparkled with clean glass, the walls were whitewashed, and the rug was from Turkey like my own back home, rich red patterned and thickly warm beneath the feet. Most beautiful of all were his chairs. One was more a settle and wide enough for at least two to sit, and three others smaller were placed around the fireplace. No fire blazed, but the space was warm. The chairs were upholstered in soft dark cloth patterned in strange shapes and were cushioned in creamy velvet. I was amazed and couldn't stop staring around until Jasper came back with a tray and a platter of sweet smells.

Placing the tray on my shameful lap, he gave me both knife and fork, and told me to eat whatever part of the feast I wished. There was also a grand green glass of red wine, and the platter held three cheeses, soft white bread rolls, sugared biscuits, a pastry cup holding warm cooked meat in whipped egg, an egg hard boiled with a spoonful of parsley on top, and two slices of cold pork pie with grated onions and spicy pickle.

I ate and drank the lot, and while I ate, Jasper talked. When I could, even if I was spitting crumbs, I answered, gulping every shred of what I'd been given.

He watched me, sitting on the chair opposite, arms loose over the chair's cushioned sides with his legs stretched before him, ankles crossed. After watching me for some time, he said, "I presume you have run from your husband?"

And I said a muffled, "Yes. He – he tied me in the shed."

Jasper lifted one eyebrow. "Is that his normal behaviour?"

Spluttering into my glass of wine, I managed, "Yes. Well, not really. He accused me of poisoning him. That was when he was disgustingly drunk after you came. A bit later he locked me in the shed. He hates me, probably as much as I hate him. And, well, I'd had the courage to say no to him. Not that one word usually stopped anything."

"Have you killed him?" Jasper asked with only slight curiosity. I just shook my head. Did he really think I could do that? Perhaps he thought I should have. Then he said, "I might kill him myself. In the meantime, you may stay here. The bedchamber upstairs is comfortable enough. There is sufficient wood behind the grate if you are cold, which no doubt you are."

I nodded again. Finally, I said, "This food is wonderful. Do you have a cook?"

"I have a wife," he said, "but at present she is away. Although," and here he smiled again, looking at me more closely, "not far away."

I blushed. I had wanted him so very badly in the past and had made a fool of myself. He could have thought me a slattern. If so, he'd shown no sign of it but he had certainly turned me down. Simply faithful to his wife, perhaps, loving her and not me. Yet he seemed entirely unconcerned and refilled my glass from a decanter on a shelf behind me. As I gulped down the last dregs of everything, I mumbled, "But if your wife returns while I am sleeping in her bed, she would be furious. And rightly so."

Now he shook his head. "You are – let us say – not unknown to her. She will understand. But first, before you soil the bedding, I suggest a bath."

That was exactly what I needed. "Please," I said. "Is there water I can boil? I'll fetch it from the well if you have a tub and bucket."

"There is a half barrel I shall bring in here, and there is water which I can heat – by another system." His smile seemed secretive. "I shall also light the fire, or you will feel the cold more once you step out."

I couldn't explain how grateful I was, and just kept saying thank you while watching his preparations. He lit the fire with his back to me, but I was interested as it seemed to take no more than a blink. The half barrel bath was quickly filled and the water steamed. The steam clouded up by the ceiling beams and the whole room began to heat in glorious welcome. The steamy swelter was the most wonderful thing I'd experienced in months.

So the bath tub stood there ready, the fire blazed, and I stood, waiting for him to leave the room.

"If you discard those remains of clothing," he said, turning to me, "I shall bring you others. My wife will not mind, and you are roughly the same size and height."

I blushed again. "I cannot believe any woman would want

that," I said, half whisper. But I had to admit it would be an enormous help. So I added, "I will leave these rags on the floor to burn after my bath, sir."

He smiled again. "So, my dear Sarah," he said as quietly as always, "please undress now while I bring you soap and towels. It will not take long."

"You?" I stared at him. I was wishing the impossible once more.

His smile suddenly glittered in his eyes like candle flames, but it was just, I think, the reflection from the fire. He said, "I have already seen you half naked, little one. But I will not interrupt your bath. While you wash, I shall amuse myself elsewhere, but will return with the clothes you need, and take those you cannot wear again."

So I waited until he brought me the hard cake of white soap, and the folded towels in a heap which he left beside the fire. When he disappeared again, I hurriedly undressed and climbed into the bliss of scalding hot water. I watched as the mud swam from my body to float at the water's surface, and then dissolve, turning my bath grey. I tried to wash my hair, gobbled dirty and soap scammed water, but sat up cleaner than I had been since Arthur threw me into the shed. But in the heat, there was just the oozing mess of memories from Arthur's attacks. and then even those I was able to wash away, one by one.

The delight continued, and the water, although now discoloured, did not even seem to cool. The fire, perhaps, kept it hot. But then as I sat so comfortably, casually watching the strings of my hair floating around my shoulders, I heard the door open with a faint click, and my head jerked upwards.

Jasper stood with a pile of neatly folded clothes in his arms. I know I blushed although hardly anything of my nakedness could be seen since I sat with water almost to my neck, and as grubby as if it was dark ale.

Then I felt the warmth of his hand beneath my chin. "Look at me," he commanded. I stared up, unflinching. His eyes were tunnels again. They enclosed me, and I disappeared into his warmth, seemingly even hotter than my bath. His eyes were the strangest I had ever seen, both loving and cold in the same moment. I imagined his gaze slipping into mine like a wolf into a cave where it knew living food hid in the shadows. I sat very still. No bubble pricked the water's surface. I hoped for more, but said nothing.

Then he said, "You must not fear me, for it is your husband I shall hurt, and only that because he must be cleaned in a different bath than yours. He must be washed free of the demon residing as his friend within."

I stuttered a yes, and asked, "He is a demon, then? A real demon?"

"Your husband is a mortal man, but the demon sucks at him from inside," Jasper said. "Now, when you have climbed from this tub, and I think the appropriate moment has cone, my dear, and when you are dressed, and eaten, drunk, and made your own decisions, I will travel through the forest and speak with your husband at your home. Do you wish to stay here, or would you accompany me? I can swear that he will neither lay hands on you, nor force you back under his authority. My wife will not return for several days, therefore you'll not meet her if you remain. However, I believe you will benefit by returning to your home at my side."

Not at all sure, since both possibilities seemed so sweet, I finally said, "If I come too, I believe you'd protect me. But once you've gone, he'll do what he wants."

Jasper shook his head. "I'll not leave you alone with Arthur. But the choice is yours."

In a way I was sure I'd be happier sleeping here, but I said, "I'll come. I want to see what he does. I want to hear what you say to him."

Again, he left me and I climbed from the tub, trying not to splash my dirty water onto his nice rug, and sat beside the fire to dry myself. With constantly repetitious stupidity I kept wondering if he would come in and help me, imagining his hands within the towel. I both felt relieved, and yet bitterly disappointed when he did not.

Now naked and aware of my own body in the firelight I saw the old and newer bruises, scars, and signs of other injuries. *At least*, I thought, *I've avoided the humiliation of Jasper seeing what a wreck I am.*

The towels he had given me were both larger and thicker yet softer than anything I had seen used like this before. His possessions were magic, almost every one. As magic as his eyes, his hands, and his words. But I called myself a fool, rubbed at my hair until it began to stop dripping and returned to its own colour, and then dressed myself in Mistress Fairweather's clothes. They were a little tight on me and I realised she was the slimmer. I couldn't take the blame for that, since it had been another demand from my husband. "*Fatten up, skinny bone-witch. I want your arse like a cream cake to eat, and your belly like a pudding to punch.*"

Tight, but beautiful and I fingered them with wonder for although I had always worn grand clothes, I had never known such soft fabric nor such glorious decoration. No Puritan then, Mistress Fairweather. And now that I would return to my husband in company with this tall proud man, I would not shiver in Puritan clothes either.

CHAPTER NINETEEN

When we set off, I wore the clothes of Jasper's wife which fitted me and which Jasper chose. Petticoats of fresh white linen, stockings of dark silk, shoes of black leather to the ankles and lined in white fleece, warm as a hot brick in bed. The gown was tight waisted in mahogany brown with a velvet stripe down each sleeve. A mahogany brown cap kept my newly washed and combed hair tucked up in the neatly pinned style, and over my gown I wore a cloak, dark blue and lined in pale blue dyed fleece. I felt well dressed, but my hat was not the humble female's starched white cap, and I had no apron and was not as prim as I should have been.

Jasper had two beautiful horses, and we galloped back towards my home on the outskirts of London's north pastures, quick as the wind until I felt we flew. Thinking of the days it had taken me to walk, lost and starving, I laughed when we arrived in just a few hours.

The grooms looked amazed, but took our horses as we dismounted, and strode to the wide door and its brass doorbell. Jasper rang the bell as if a warning of fire. The butler answered, and I marched inside without a word, with Jasper following, uninvited. I led him into the large living chamber and shrugged off the cape. Jasper removed his coat and shook out his lace cuffs. Wearing no wig, his hair was wind ruffled, but now he shook it back as he also removed his hat, passing these discarded outer garments to the butler.

"Tell Lord Harrington that we are here and wish to speak with him," I said, and sat by the fire flaming bright across the hearth. Jasper stood, his elbow to the mantle.

It was some time before Arthur appeared. He was glaring, but straightened and smiled when he saw Jasper, nodded to me and returned to Jasper.

"Sir," he said, "I am most obliged to you for bringing my wife home to me. She is an errant and wilful female, but I am mighty glad to have my little woman home again. It is late, and you have probably travelled some distance under the circumstances. Will you take a glass of wine with me before you leave?"

Being cold but polite as usual, Jasper thanked him. I said, "I'll have some wine too," and frowned at Arthur.

He scowled back. "I think not," he said. "I believe you should retire to your bedchamber, madam. I wish to speak in private to our friend."

I had no intention of being locked away again. I shook my head. "No," I said. "The wine would be a great comfort, considering I intend staying here and joining the conversation."

Arthur stepped forwards, both hands clenched, ready to order me out, but Jasper interrupted. "I believe, my lord, that your wife should remain. Sarah has been – let us say – unwell. She has a great deal to say. And you might think that this is not my business. Yet, I have no doubt, I may be of some assistance to you both."

My vile husband managed several different furious expressions one after the other, and then coughed, marching over to sit by us. "Very well," he said. "But I must tell you at the outset, sir, that my wife is a woman of sin and promiscuity. She rarely speaks the truth and has assuredly been telling you lies ever since she met you. I will have her punished according to our Lord Protector's new regime, but as always, I shall be lenient."

I almost laughed. Jasper, still standing, smiled. "My lord, I have come to know your wife a little better over these past months. Although I have met with her on relatively few occasions, I can tell quite easily whether or not she tells me the truth. For example, she came to me this day wearing the ruined remnants of old clothes. It was also quite obvious that she was excessively hungry and had been walking alone for many days, which involved sleeping under the trees. I will not believe any woman would choose to behave in this manner, suffering both the fear and the cold discomfort, unless for some exceptionally important reason. We have spoken at length. Now I wish to know why you imprisoned your wife without food or comfort and punished her consistently."

Although Jasper was as still as a statue, his eyelids were half closed. His eyes were both narrowed and coldly menacing. I knew menace when I saw it, even when the threat came from someone not waving a whip.

Arthur almost choked. Abruptly he stood and faced Jasper staring up at him, in anger. Being much shorter, Arthur strained his neck, then glowered back at me.

"These are lies," he said loudly. "I would never and have never done any such thing. She ran away to one of her other lovers, and clearly that other man has mistreated her. Master Fairweather, I deny ever hurting any female. Certainly, I must punish her now as the law demands, but I would never lock her away nor deny her food."

"Why, then would she run from you?" Jasper asked softly.

"Because she is a minx," Arthur shouted back.

The tray, the glasses and the wine decanter had been brought and I was drinking with determination. It fired my courage. Arthur was drinking heavily as well. Jasper sipped, looking bored. Perhaps it wasn't the best wine, but I wouldn't have known. We must have been nearing midnight, and I wondered if he'd change his mind and leave me here, half pissed and vulnerable as he rode back home.

But he kept his promise.

He said, always softly, "Although I cannot believe your words, my lord, I can sympathise." Arthur jerked backwards in fury, but Jasper continued. "I have known many men who fail to discover pleasure without enacting perversions or indulging in cruelty. But there are ways of countering this. Indeed, there are ways of bringing far greater happiness into a life and finding the relief of affection, after permitting the removal of – such an impulse. Some call it killing the demon."

I smiled but turned my face away. Arthur stamped both feet. "Rubbish, sir. If anyone here could be described as a demon, it is her." He pointed with one shuddering finger. 'This trollop is the witch. Our church preaches the truth of damnation, and my wife is surely damned. But I will not allow her to curse me, nor bring her wickedness into my home." Now I laughed and he nearly grabbed me.

I glared over the brim of my glass and muttered, "My home too." But caught Jasper's tiny shake of the head, and returned to my wine.

Again, Jasper stepped forwards, and taking Arthur by the shoulders, firmly guided him to the nearest chair. "I believe," he said, "you are tired, sir. I suggest brandy, since that is the tonic that will bring both peace of mind and excellence of judgement. Would you try brandy, sir?"

"Never drunk it in my life," muttered the earl. "And I see no reason to start. Besides, I don't have any."

With his usual tuck beside his mouth, Jasper resisted the

smile. "But I do," he said. "And offer it willingly. Though not for the lady, perhaps."

I almost scowled at him. Then I guessed what he meant. I'd never actually heard of brandy and had no desire to try it out, but I watched the temptation settle around Arthur's head like a halo. "Worth a try. Yes, bring it out, Master Fairweather."

With a confident flourish, Vespasian brought out a flask from inside his jacket. It was a metal bottle, rather small, and polished like silver. He leaned over, offering it to my husband, who pulled out the cork and swallowed it down with a glug of satisfaction. "Pleasant stuff," he admitted. It seemed he had almost forgotten about his errant min of a wife sitting and watching him. He gulped again, and swallowed it down, keeping a firm grasp on the flask. "Didn't expect it to be so pleasant," he added without any visible intention of returning the container. "Yes," he swigged again, "very nice indeed."

I could see the bruises I had inflicted on him myself, and hoped they hurt as much as some of my injuries did. No doubt he was dreaming of the disgusting punishments he'd deliver once Jasper had left.

Although not yet regaining his metal flask of brandy, Jasper did not complain. "In simple terms," he said, "brandy is the concentrated extract of wine. Help yourself, my lord."

And he did. He kept on drinking as Jasper and I sat cheerfully finishing our original glasses of wine.

Arthur rolled his eyes. He grinned, a mouthful of crooked teeth flashing, swigged the last drops of the brandy and wiped his mouth as a small dark dribble trickled down his chin. "Good stuff," he said with liquid enthusiasm. "Must buy some myself." He leaned back in the chair, crossed his arms with the flask still tight in one hand, and abruptly fell asleep. Within a minute he was snoring.

This had happened so fast that I was surprised, but Jasper rose and took back the flask from my husband's iron fisted grip. Clearly it was empty. Jasper tucked it again inside his jacket. "Drugged," he said without shame. "Convenient of course, since otherwise I would have needed to knock him out. I have saved my knuckles from bleeding after all. Now do as I say. Come here and hold the creature upright."

I tried to keep my drunken pig of a husband straight on his chair although he slumped most of the time and twice nearly tumbled to the rugs. Meanwhile Jasper leaned from the back and grasped Arthurs entire head between his hands, holding it so tightly that I wondered if it would crush.

"Out," demanded Jasper, speaking far more loudly than I had ever heard him before. "I have spoken to you already and you know what will happen this time if you refuse to obey."

It was as if Arthur lived again. His eyes clicked open and the pupils seemed to burn scarlet as the iris blinked bright blue. As I had seen before, it was as if the eyes spoke. The thing said, "You failed before, foolish human. You'll fail again."

"Success," Jasper said, "is a judgement and not a fact. Come out and we will compare whatever comprises our judgements of the opposition."

The eyes sniggered. "Want me out, craven liar? You come in. There's room in here for one more crap-ridden prick-sick idiot to cuddle the piss-addled drunk human already here. Make a good pair, you will. I pinch and I pull, but I'll not kill the ignorant bugger until I've had my fun."

"Your own ignorance is evident," Jasper said, almost crooning. "No human can enter another. To face me, you must come out. Or you are the craven drunk. Have you shared the brandy?"

"Why come out, when you see me clear, and I see you. I'm stronger than you'll ever be, human idiot."

"So sad perhaps," Jasper answered, his voice soft again. "But I cannot pity you for the ignorance. Clearly you do not know the game I play."

"What?" demanded the eyes at once.

"I cannot feed you," Jasper replied, "while you are immersed within another."

"If I come out, you take me in?" The demon voice seemed confused.

Tightening his clasp on Arthur's head, Jasper pressed both thumbs to the temples, and although deeply unconscious, Arthur whined. It hurt him.

I no longer needed to hold the wretch upright, and I sat, elbows on my knees, watching closely. I did not really know what was happening, but while watching and guessing, I supposed it was a form of exorcism. Yet I also knew that the beautiful Jasper was no priest. He acted with force, not with holy words or the raising of a small and holy cross. There was no torture, no cruelty and no anger. But this very secret exorcism was to be achieved by force.

Arthur's momentary pain gave me a spiteful sting of pleasure. Of course, I hoped none of the staff would come this time and guessed they would mostly be in bed. Even the butler's bedtime had passed, unless he was called. And he certainly wasn't going to be called.

Jasper continued, "The man you suck is a tyrant. Do you enjoy exaggerating a fool already as wicked as yourself? Or do you claim credit for the man's entire range of talents?"

"Why not?" demanded the demon. "I gobbled him when he was young, miserable little bugger. And it was me as gave him his appetites and his greedy tastes. Jollied himself in the usual human way, he did, when I found him and ate half his brain. He's mine now, and I sit with joy when the bastard fucks his wife the only way he wants now I've eaten him from inside. And I ain't leaving. You want me with you instead? Not interested, big boy. I's happy as a louse in here."

"And if I kill the man you occupy? You will float freely but cold, needing to find another home more apt than before."

"Plenty folks ready out there," sniggered the voice.

But now Jasper pressed one hand down on the top of Arthur's head, while the other hand slipped around his scrawny neck. "Out now," Jasper breathed hot into Arthur's ear. There was a scream, so shocking that I thought the staff would hear and come rushing. But the scream was swallowed back, and no one came.

Those demon eyes sparked crimson flames.

"Don't try no tricks on me, pathetic human," it said. "You can't copy my riches, mortal boy. Go find another human to haunt."

But immediately Jasper opened Arthur's mouth, thrusting it wide with four of his fingers. And then he leaned forwards and began to breathe into my husband's throat. He blew hot air, and I saw something glisten with pain in those demonic eyes. I kept watching, and the thing's eyes kept shrinking. I think it was a long time. We had no clock and nothing chimed from the corridor outside. But perhaps time stood still. Watching, blinking hard, it looked to me as if Jasper almost kissed that open gaping mouth of Arthur's, lips to lips. Yet the snap of teeth to teeth and the cold power in Jasper's eyes proved the gigantic and terrifying difference.

And then, eventually there was a vile stink and a plume of leprous green tinged cloud swooped from Arthur's mouth.

"More," commanded Jasper, and blew again.

The rest of the slime coated cloud, a stagnant mist and another stench carrying a stream of decay and sour wickedness, spilled from Arthur's throat and puddled across the floor. Yet it rose, taking cloud shape, and then spread, tapering into fog-dark fingers.

Turning quickly, Jasper muttered under his breath. I had no

idea what he said, nor could I understand the words. But the filth swirled downwards, and the fingers began to shrink.

One, slug-like, wriggled forwards and pointed at me. I hid my face.

Now, floating within the fog but sinking as if its weight pulled it down, a fading voice of fury swore and cursed. "Human frog-worm," it said, struggling to find its voice, "Shit-mouth and piss-eyes, you dare blow angel-dust into my purity? I shall suck you empty of all humanity and claw your pretty skin from your face."

But the words faded as though coming from a great distance, and once again Jasper, still gripping that ugly head, spoke the charm he had used before. The sound of it seemed beautiful to me, like music or a hymn from the old church. I listened closely although understood nothing.

But hearing those words, the ghostly fingers had gone and only one remained. Jasper blew and the finger became cloud, the cloud became grit and the grit fell to the floorboards.

Jasper ground the tiny grains beneath his heel. A faint whimpering faded. Jasper continued to press the heel of his boots until the whining had quite gone. Then he looked down. One tiny red seed, smaller than a grape pip, sat unmoving on his hand. Pressing it between his finger and thumb nail, Jasper again murmured words I could not recognise. The red seed completely disappeared.

Arthur continued to sleep but his eyes were his own again and they were tight closed. Over the chair and my husband's inert body, Jasper looked at me.

My heart leapt.

Then softly he said, "You are not yet free, my dear. The demon is gone and no other wickedness can enter for some time to come. But your husband has consumed demonic lust for many years, and will not awake suddenly kind. He does not understand love and never will. So shall I leave you here with him, or stay to protect you?"

In my bed, perhaps? "No," I said, though without conviction. "Please go back to your wife. Apologise to her for my theft of her clothes, but give her thanks from my heart, and tell her I am so very grateful both to her – and to her remarkable husband. I will sleep now, and barricade my door until the morning."

Jasper leaned against the inside of the door, ready to leave me. Shutting Arthur's door behind us, Jasper walked with me along the corridor towards the stairs.

"I should return your wife's clothes," I said.

"She will neither miss them, nor care," he murmured. "And Arthur will not search for you. He cannot wake for many hours. But when he does, he'll be riddled with the remainder of the venom within the brandy I gave him. At first, he will fall, still doped, and remember nothing. Then he'll become a mixture of fury, fear and memory. And once gone, I will not be able to return to help you. Yet," and his smile widened in the fading firelight, "I am quite sure that you will manage very well indeed without me."

"I'm – tired," I muttered and turned away, hugging myself as though bitterly cold.

But he came behind me and caught my wrists between his hands, stopping me. And looking down at me, shook his head, speaking so very, very softly into my ear. "The woman who is so like you, who is almost within you is my wife. And because I adore her, I feel drawn to you. Yet to say I love you would be untrue, and I do not welcome falsity into my life. I do not know you well, little one, and you know me not at all. My wife knows you better, although that may seem absurd. However, I wish you happiness, and trust that you discover true love one day, which will stretch far beyond the lust you feel for me."

He had gone. I understood and darted back up the stairs to

my bedchamber. I lit no candles. My bed chamber was dark, the shutters up and no fire alight. I lay on my bed and cried.

Yet then, between my tears and the cold creases of my bed beneath me, I became aware of something that was as magical as Jasper always seemed, and yet was not frightening at all. The whisper I heard was in my head, and it was a woman who spoke to me.

"He loves you, in a way," soothed the voice. "We are together, you and I. Jasper is a part of me and I am a part of you. This means that Jasper is also a part of you."

I quivered with excitement, as if I was hearing an angel's prophesies. I whispered back, though silently and in my thoughts where the other voice lay. "Will I ever know love again? With him or another?"

The voice continued. "Not with him for he does not belong in your time and must leave to return into his own future. But you will meet a man you love, and he will love you in return."

I lay there afterwards, breathing deeply, unable to speak.

CHAPTER TWENTY

B liss to be myself and not that other self. I was Molly again, I wondered what Sarah would think of me if only we could meet, but that was a very bad and unlikely idea.

But there wasn't much time to laugh, even with myself. I was stomping, wet and muddy, across the open plains beyond the school and its clumping trees.

The well had been cleaned, emptied down to its deepest level of incoming water, was pronounced safe to drink, and no longer stank out the nearby village. I was not so sure, and if I really had to drink from it, I made sure to boil the water first.

William's decaying corpse was examined by the sheriff's interesting assistant, and then buried. I knew it was William and of course Agnes knew it was William, but it could not be proved and the mangled flesh and bones were buried without identity. Agnes told me she had no regrets, yet refused to speak any more about it. I confess I didn't care about William's death for his own sake, only for the strengthening demon that Agnes housed.

Tom understood none of it and had no idea that his aunt had committed the fascinating slaughter which had got the whole school talking, before half of the boys were promptly removed to safer places by their shocked parents. Some stayed. After all, over past years there had been so much fighting and death over the country, one more made little difference.

Getting hold of Agnes and pulling out the demon as Vespasian had was not going to be on my list of talents. Getting her asleep without waking was beyond me, let alone anything more. But I was determined to try, had planned it over and over, and the one thing I might do first was to find William's bodyless head, and see if it might prove its killer.

I had searched the whole school of course, including ovens, the loft, under beds, and in the back of cupboards. Then I had searched the grounds. There were plenty of bushes and trees to rummage through, but no drips of blood nor chopped heads appeared.

I walked further. The open fields about a half mile south from the school were turning boggy for the weather was worsening. Constantly wet, cold and icy, one morning I had awoken believing it had snowed heavily in the night. I stood enchanted at the window gazing at the pure white stretching out into an invisible horizon. But when I hurried downstairs and peered from the doorway at what lay outside, I realised it was only frost. But a frost so white and solid, it seemed as thick as snow. Indeed, when I walked across it to the well, it crunched and cracked underfoot as though I was breaking pieces of china.

Then, at the far end of one of the fields where a stubby hedge separated each plot from another, I discovered a mass of black sticky substance, which had collected in just one area. I looked up, and there the head sat, spiked on the bare winter branches of a lilac bush. The eyes were open, glazed and staring and since the mouth gaped open too, it seemed as though William Prestwich was chortling at the world around.

The neck was a stump of reeking flesh, festooned with blistering veins and arteries, sinews and whatever else the rotting flesh contained still, hanging like slimy ribbons from the neck. I looked away quickly. It was monstrous and I was nearly sick. It was also clear that some form of torture had been attempted, since large symmetrical holes opened each cheek, and the teeth inside the open mouth seemed to have been broken or removed by force.

Stumbling back to the school, I was both disgusted and disappointed for nothing seemed to relate back to Agnes. Yet in spite of her demon, it was a greater monster she had murdered, and so I tried to ignore the vile circumstances, and simply reported my discovery to Henry.

Back came the sheriff and back came his assistant, and off I strode once again to stand beneath that knotted bush, avoiding the hard-black puddles below, and pointed up to the horror above. The head was identified and taken away first for examination and secondly to be buried with the body. We all attended the funeral, and although a Puritan funeral was quiet enough, I couldn't help feeling that William didn't deserve such pure sympathy. Agnes was there too. I talked to her afterwards. As usual, she was unhelpful.

"I ain' talking no more," she told me, poking grey strands of hair up under her white starched cap. "You bloody knows it were me. So hop it, and stop poking your nose in where it ain't wanted."

But this time I lay back against the one tiny flat pillow on my bed, crossed my arms and regarded her with a hypocritical smile. "The head was a gruesome surprise," I lied cheerfully. "Why did you knock out his teeth?"

She turned away in silence as usual, but then I heard her muttering, saying, "The bugger tried to bite me. Bloody big bite too. Didn't deserve teeth, did he!"

When I said, "Good. Didn't deserve his life, either," she turned back to me and her face lost the secretive glower.

"You really wanna know wot happened? And you swear you won't tell no one?"

Could I lie to that extent? Probably yes, so I answered, "Yes, I really want to know. And would I be so daft as to spread the story around? Besides," I added, "there's no proof it was you."

Perhaps she'd been dying to tell someone, so Agnes sat on her bed facing me and talked for ages, telling me far more than I wanted.

"Out there in the fields one night, it were. Stars. But black, and bloody cold. Well, the little lad I used to fondle often when I was lonely, he weren't to be found. Not nowhere. So I took another lad by the hand. I'd had him before, and he weren't easy but I threatened the usual stuff and off we went."

I gulped. Staring, open mouthed, I began to think I should kill her as she had killed William. Not just the demon, but Agnes too. I mumbled, "You do that often?"

"Not as often as that other bugger," Agnes exclaimed. "So anyway, little Percy and me, we walked over the field where no bugger could be seen from the school, 'til I heard a whole load of squeaks and whining, like kicking a stray dog. And there were bloody creepy William with my own lad."

"Tom?" I gasped.

"No, no." She sounded contemptuous. "The lad with the yellow curls what I always did when I could. He liked a bit o' cuddling, and if he didn't like all the suck and blow, he just did as he were told and shut up. But William were hurting him far more n' I ever did. So I shouted at the bastard, and he let the brat go. He pulled up his braces and ran off quick with Percy, cos I let him go too. Then I marched up to William and gave him a good kick. He swore at me and kicked back. Well, that started it, and we fought. Right viscous, he were, but I had a bloody good carving knife and a hammer too, seeing as I never brought a lad out for night play without a way o' fighting off spies, other kids or wild animals. Well, this time it were a wild animal, for that's what William were. I did him after a long scramble, and stuck me knife in his belly, right up to the handle. But he didn't piss off dead right away. Slow loss of blood, it were. So I did a few things first like making holes in his face with the point of the knife, and banging out the bugger's teeth with me hammer. Then I slammed the hammer into the top of his head, and that were it. Dead forever. I'd lost a chunk of me leg where he bit me bloody hard, and he nearly bit me finger off too. I weren't well fer a long time. Anyway, the bastard had gone. So couldn't tell on me, couldn't swive no more little boys, and couldn't take the ones I like meself."

"But if you - " I stammered.

She knew what I meant. "But I kisses and cuddles the lads,' she said. sighing. "Then, when I tells 'em what to do to me, I's gentle and I gives 'em pennies and apples. William – he hurt the brats real mean. So 'tis mighty different."

I wasn't at all sure about that, but I sighed and lay still before saying, "Have you ever killed anyone else?"

"Only my first intended," she said without any sign of shame. "He were a good deal older n' me when I was just a lass. I think I were around fourteen. He took me cherry o'course and then swived me over and over. We done promised one to the other, saying them words wot meant we was to wed proper soon. But after a couple o' months he told me he didn't want me as wife, and he'd be off in the morning. So I killed the bugger. Right there and then, wiv me fist to the bastard's prick and me kitchen knife to his ear. I got a good grip, and it went in right slippery. After all, I'd bin using it to clean a chicken's innards so it were already drippin' wiv guts. No harm there."

"Um," I said.

"Mind you," she added, "his prick where I punched the bugger, were a right tiddly little thing. But I didn't knows that 'till later."

"I – see," I mumbled, although I didn't.

"And now you knows it all," grinned Agnes. "Reckon I can show you som'thing else. Real pretty it is." I was prepared for something disgusting, but actually this particular souvenir didn't occur to me before she pulled out the wrapped package from beneath her pillow. She chucked it at me, and I managed to catch the little brown paper parcel. It wasn't heavy. I started to pull open the paper.

And then there in my lap lay a slightly elongated scrap of flesh. At first, I thought it was a finger. But then I realised there were no knuckles and indeed, no bones inside at all. And beneath the inch of dried muck, there was a larger lump which also seemed to be flesh. The smaller and longer piece lay on the round, but larger. And that was when I realised what this was. I had touched it before understanding so then pulling back, I found my own fingers trembling.

"Is this what I think it is?"

"I cut it off him afore I smashed his head in, so the bastard felt it go. I kept it fer fun. Reckon I'll chuck it soon, it don't do me no good. But I reckon it brings me great dreams."

"I just think it sounds disgusting." It smelled disgusting too.

"True, fer that bugger were disgusting," she said. "So I used the saw the gardener uses to coppice the trees, and I pulled his ugly head off. But he didn't feel naught fer he were already total dead."

I had a sudden glimpse of my garden's trees blowing without wind, and heaved. After gathering my wits, I said, "Do you have a headache, Agnes? I could – soothe it. I mean, stroking your head. I've done it before and so I know it works."

Of course I was remembering Vespasian's magic calling of the demon, but she stared at me with the usual contempt. "You thinks you're some healer or sommint? Careful lass, the idiots'll call you a witch and hang you from the gibbet."

"No, not like that," I gulped. "But it's soothing, and it helps. Anyway, shall we give it a try?"

"I ain't got no bloody headache," Agnes replied, lying flat and stretching out her legs.

"You're going to sleep?" I asked hopefully.

But she grunted again. "No, lass, not yet. 'Tis a mite early. But reckon I could day-dream a twitch or so, remembering that bastard down the well."

Reluctantly I sat on her bed, pushing up on the pillow behind her head. I honestly didn't like touching her, especially since she stank of dirt and sweat, even though I probably did too. I was nervous in case she decided that any gentle touch to her head might mean I wanted a good deal more. But with determination, I said, "Look, I can relax you. Yes, dream away. Then tell me if you feel better afterwards."

I placed my hands carefully around her head the way Vespasian had always started his magical call to the demons inside, but quickly found that my much smaller hands did not stretch to the whole circumference. Yet I persisted. I began to press my hands, thumbs to her temples. Her hair was slick with grease and her forehead was grubby, but I tried to ignore such unimportant details, and pressed again.

Agnes sat up abruptly, slapping my hands away, and glared at me. "Silly bitch," she shouted. "Wot yer doing? I says no before. You wanna climb into bed with me or something? Well, no, bitch. I ain't interested in other females, and not you in particular. Just a skinny interfering idiot, you is. So bugger off or you'll end up down the well and all."

My courage, my determination and my good intentions all flew away like the robins in spring. And quickly I smiled, for it was just as well. I'd have made a mess of it and possibly given the demon a laugh. Vespasian, on the other hand, would have laughed for a different reason.

CHAPTER TWENTY-ONE

I called Vespasian but he was hard to contact and I knew why. If he was beside Sarah, or deep in political conversation with Cromwell – or anyone else if it came to that – he was too deeply into the time zone and was hidden to me. I didn't belong in the 1650s and was simply a time traveller, here because of Vespasian's power. I slipped into Sarah's mind and found her deeply content, and deeply asleep. No way I could creep into Cromwell's mind and nor did I wish to. His sort of blind rigidity had fostered cruelty before the demon had even fostered his fanaticism and willingness to hurt in order to overcome.

I therefore left Agnes alone until the next night when she cheerfully swallowed a mug of ale spiced with sedative. I hoped Vespasian would hear my call, and could come to kill off our last demon. He had already told me what had happened to the others. Once this was achieved, we could go home. I very much wanted to go and see Randle again and relax in my own house. I dreamed of cuddling Randle, and of Vespasian cuddling me.

He came. From our tiny attic dormitory, I saw my beautiful husband from the window. he stood in the grounds, gazing out at the night sky, his back to me. In the next narrow bed beside mine, Agnes was deeply asleep. The remaining maid, since others had quickly left, had gone home to Mamma for Sunday and would not return until Monday morning. Agnes snoring was the only sound, so I opened the bedroom window and whistled. Vespasian turned. He was grinning, nodded, and slipped through the door into the kitchens, quickly finding his way up the stairs to the loft.

I heard an owl call as I closed the window, then saw the silent stretch of its mottled wings. I sighed, turned to look at Agnes, and waited for Vespasian to climb the three sets of narrow stairs.

When he came into the room, I whispered the latest news and the confession that Agnes had related, and told him I had drugged her with Vespasian's own special recipe. He sat on the edge of the mattress beside her, and instantly began the same procedure which he had explained to me before.

"There are always differences," he said as he wrapped his hands around her brow. "Each creature is an individual, and those amongst us who have been impregnated are vastly varying characters. But let us see what this woman houses."

Agnes wore a petticoat-shift in bed, and her grey hair was loose, tangled across the pillow. The blanket was tucked up beneath her arms, and as she snored, mouth open, a tiny shred of pink caressed her rotting teeth and trickled onto her tongue.

Squeezing the palms of his hands tighter, Vespasian spoke softly as always, calling, "I should like to meet you. Will you come out?"

The shreds of wafting pink gossamer rushed tightly together as if forming a barrier. Then a soft voice, pretty and even alluring, crooned. "Oh, my lord, I am flattered. But I dare not leave my mother."

I smiled. I hadn't really expected a female, still a monster as it was, and a flirtatious demon seemed ludicrous. Vespasian seemed less surprised, but I doubt if he'd really expected this reply either.

His thumbs inched towards the temples, and Agnes snored louder. "I offer no choices," Vespasian said. "I come here only to speak with you, and not for the woman you inhabit. Come out and talk with me."

"I can see you," said the childish voice. "I can speak with you and hear you very well indeed. There is absolutely no gain in my making some unnecessary appearance. So, delightful as I find you, my lord, I do not wish to leave my mother."

"Do you speak with your mother?" I couldn't help asking, even though I was probably interrupting Vespasian.

The squeaky answer sounded less attractive. "No. Of course not. How ignorant."

So I kept my mouth shut.

Vespasian was patient. Although he tensed his fingers and kept his hands firm around the head, thumbs pressing on the temples, he spoke as though there was all the time without the slightest need to hurry. He said, "So you do not wish to explore the world, nor the welcoming souls of the other humans around. Some would no doubt be better suited to you." He shrugged. "The choice is yours, although I could force you if I wished."

After a slight pause, the thing said, "Why do you want me out? What good would it do either of us?" The thing seemed to titter, high pitched. "Oh my, my, handsome man, do you wish to kiss me? I am attractive, I know, but I do not kiss strangers. Only my mother."

"I am a teacher of spirit," Vespasian said, which was true enough in one way. "There are many opportunities which you are missing. But I may move on to another more accessible than yourself."

Another short silence, and then the creature answered in a voice less puerile and more masculine than before. "Perhaps I understand your predicament. But you are a human and cannot therefore understand mine. I prefer females to infiltrate. They are more delightful to influence in unique ways. I eat their dreams of romance, and change them into the details of sexual depravity. So much more enjoyable, as I presume you must know. Debauch, deprave, experiment first, then plunge into your grave. Already since I was set free from Lilith's symbolic prison, I have devoured five humans and six weaker demons. But floating entirely free simply to speak regarding alternatives, when I am so utterly content with what I already have, seems somewhat pointless. I sit snug here, and the cradle fits me so neatly, I hear my mother's heartbeat, and that is like the music of Hell's pathways. She tries to kiss me within when I tickle her crotch. I want no other opportunities and will not leave this new mother of mine until she dies."

"Perhaps I should not disclose the world's secrets," Vespasian replied with calm persistence. "But this female will be dying very soon. I am giving you the chance to leave before she leaves this world."

With considerable hesitation, the thing said, "You offer me a kind choice? I am unaccustomed to kindness from humans. I am doubtful. Are you sincere? Are you to be trusted?"

"Ask her," Vespasian indicated me as I stood there beside him. "She trusts me."

"Does she want me?" it asked. "Is this one of your alternatives?"

I quickly backed away.

"I have other adventures in mind," Vespasian said. "This woman is meek and kind-hearted. She would give you no pleasure."

"But I prefer females," it said again. "They are imaginative, and so many seem meek until you enter, and find that within they yearn to shout and scream, to hurt and enslave, and most of all to kill. So many wish to kill their husband or their master, their lord of the manor, or their father. Sometimes even the son. I find great enjoyment in helping with such wishes. If not this female, then find me another."

"I know many female humans suitable," Vespasian said, with a quick grin at me. "But whether your intense colouration would suit them, I cannot tell."

"I adore being pink," it complained. "I'm not changing. Go stuff yourself with some other silly idea."

"However," Vespasian sighed, "if you came out, instead of hiding like some cowardly symbol, I might help you dye your tones either deeper, for a stronger appeal, or fainter for a more feminine beauty."

After some thought, the voice again became masculine. "Bugger off," it said suddenly. "I can stay whatever colour I like. Pink ain't seen much in this age. It attracts the females. Did I tell you I like females best? Yes, reckon I did. So piss off, slime-arse and go nibble your own shit."

Abruptly and without warning, Vespasian bent, snapped the ugly mouth further open and ignoring the nasal snores and the guttural echoes, he placed his lips inside Agnes's and blew so furiously that I had to shut my own mouth hard to stifle the gasp.

He continued to blow. The demon said nothing, and appeared to be hanging on with difficulty, for faint pink wisps rose from the throat, wafting around Vespasian's teeth.

Then the sounds from within the sleeping woman began to whine and then cry. A faint voice murmured, "I thought you kind. But you are cruel."

"Are you kind?" Vespasian asked. "Or are you cruel?" And he blew again, even harder. The shivering threads untangled and curled alone, dithering, attempting to cling, before being swept from the open mouth and flying up into the air high above the beds. And as Vespasian blew without rest, so the pink mist oozed from Agnes like some surrendering dream.

Now Vespasian's breath was shaded pink, mixing with the

cloud blossoming outwards, and the air about us was as pink as rosebuds. I shut my mouth and clasped both hands over it. I didn't want to breathe demon into my lungs. And one blink after I had swallowed that thought, the gritty cloud burst outwards and surged towards me. My hands already covered my face except for my eyes, and now all I could see was the froth of the unbodied demon, which closely entwined around me, which looked and smelled like vomit.

Now Vespasian was blowing around my face, and under his breath he was speaking words I decided must be Latin, but could not understand them. I buried my face in my lap, leaning over in desperation, my hands covering what I could, and then the material of my skirts. I could still smell the filth and slime and I could still hear Vespasian's voice and the passionate exhalation of his breath.

I think he said, "Et abiit iam et desitis exprobramini"

It was probably Latin, but I had no idea what it meant. I was too busy cringing and wanting to be sick again. But Vespasian was never prepared to fail. With an echoing explosion, he clapped his hands, and as the pink mist dispersed into threads once more, he blew ever more fiercely.

Another switch – and the cloud was grit and the grit muffled my nose and breathing since my mouth was already covered tight shut, and I knew I had demon grit finding its way into my head. Vespasian grabbed me. Now he was blowing into my mouth, and it suddenly felt as sweet as a kiss. The grit tumbled from my face and scattered across the floor. Vespasian dropped me, which was strangely uncomfortable, as he stamped hard across the floor. Pink wisps rose, then disintegrated once more, and the stench of death and decay was as strong and as vile as that from the corpse in the well.

Now finally a heaped pile of the grit scattered. Then it lost colour and shrank into no more than dust. Piece by tiny piece, it popped with little smelly sparks that left only a very few minute grains behind. But evidently even the dust had to be removed or it could regenerate. I sat very still, holding my breath, and not daring to move.

There was no sound at all except the crunching of my husband's feet on the floor boards. It seemed a long time, and I was worried that the thumping would disturb whoever slept below the attic room, but no one interrupted us. And eventually after the stench had blown away, the air smelled fresh and no cloud, mist or flecks of any kind remained, Vespasian bent and retrieved one tiny bead of red from the floor, so small I was surprised he could see it. He rubbed this between his forefinger and thumb, and spoke two more words beneath his breath.

So now even the intangible memory of the demon had gone.

"Now she is free of the thing," Vespasian said. "She will wake in an hour or two, but the demon is dead and cannot re-create. And so there are no longer twelve creatures outside our home. There are nine. Which is too many. But my strength is the greater, and I can eliminate nine whereas conquering all fourteen together may have been too much of a challenge. I am, after all, short on practise."

I gazed at him with absolute admiration. "You are – magic," I whispered. "And I adore you so very, very much. Can we go home now to Randle?"

"We can," Vespasian said softly. "But there are three things we should do first."

I couldn't think of three. "Rest?" I suggested. "Make love?"

He smiled. "Firstly, arrange a future for the boy Thomas that will not involve any demon within. A certain level of security and care should be given, if we can find such a thing."

I raised an eyebrow. "Henry Bloom, perhaps. And secondly?"

"Secondly, I must ensure the comfortable future of your

previous incarnation, my love. Sarah also needs some immediate protection."

"And thirdly?" I was still hoping he'd say make love.

Instead he said, "Thirdly will come a little later. But in the meantime, my beloved, perhaps we should kill Agnes."

CHAPTER TWENTY-TWO

I slept in Jasper's arms in the wallow of my own bed, and my own dreams. I knew I was alone, and I knew that Jasper had left me even before I slept, but I imagined him there. And that vision of twining together beneath the eiderdown and velvet coverlet seemed almost as warmly enchanting as the real thing might have been. Arthur was still drugged and unconscious. I imagined what would happen in the morning. Arthur would storm into my bedchamber, accusing me of anything he could think of. Or without the demon within, would he become kind and tolerant? Would he love me in the traditional manner, and could I ever learn to love him? I slept with the thoughts twisting, racing and shouting in my dreams.

I woke with the patter of rain against my window.

It was Jasper's final words to me before he left the previous night, which now echoed in my head. "What I want cannot always be achieved. I can no longer live in your world," Jasper had told me. And I understood completely. He was no normal man. He was a magical being, perhaps a magician or a sorcerer, even a warlock. The church, I knew, would want him dead on the gallows and yet he had helped me so much, and I am sure he helped others.

Then there had been the other voice, the woman's words, which I knew to be true even though I couldn't be sure who she was. Jasper's wife? Or some mystical spirit? Perhaps that might be the same being.

"As absolute leader of church and country," he had murmured softly, "Cromwell will continue only for five years. Less now, since his unpleasant reign of suspicion and hatred is already begun. A new regime will bring new freedoms for those who wish them, and the king's son will return. He does not forgive England for murdering his father, but he becomes a placid king. You will face a new life."

"And Arthur?" I had asked, shivering as if the ice had sneaked in beneath the door. He had stared down at me, his face was coldly expressionless, and yet I knew exactly what he was saying into my head.

"Arthur's future depends on you, my dear."

"That would be a sin indeed," I muttered.

"Self-defence," he told me, his expression unchanging, "is no sin unless you defend yourself against a body weaker than your own."

"Have you ever – killed anyone?" I asked him in a whisper.

He regarded me unblinking. "Many times." Cold-eyed. "I have killed in self-defence and I have killed in battle. But I have also killed in sin. I am no faultless hero, and I have sometimes known sin to be a blessing."

Lowering my eyes, I nodded although I wasn't sure how that would work. Perhaps, even without immediate risk, to kill a man whom you fear and who has abused you for years, would be self-defence in a way.

Jasper had kissed my cheek before he left. When the door shut behind him it felt as though the daylight had gone too, and my room was once again made of ice. Then I had embraced his memory and even though his arms had gone, they kept me warm and content throughout the night.

It was the woman's voice inside my head which calmed me more than even Jasper himself.

Walking with the pitter-patter of the light rain against my mullions, I began desperately discussing with myself the one thing I wanted to do but felt I should not. Eventually I stood and pulled on the warmth of my bed robe, then slowly walked up the corridor to my husband's bedchamber.

I sat watching Agnes, wondering what she might feel – or do – when she woke. I wished she might not wake at all, but since she was still snoring loudly, she was bound to wake at some time in the morning.

But I had seen the essence of cruelty pulled from within her and destroyed utterly. What I did not know, is what difference that would make to her character. I had an idea that it would make little difference, perhaps some, but after ingesting such growing wickedness for so long, and cheerfully becoming what it was itself, I could not believe that the woman herself could change now.

Yet we came to destroy the demons at a stage earlier in their progression, and have done exactly that," Vespasian reminded me. "We did not come to kill those humans left after the demons have gone, even though any world would gain from their disappearance."

I turned to Vespasian. He sat beside me, his arm around my shoulders, his hand in my hair as I rested my head against him.

"I've never killed anyone as myself," I said. "Except when I –

became - another sort of demon. I don't pretend to understand that part of the past. But killing Agnes is a temptation."

"As always, you are free," he said. It was a somewhat casual statement considering I was talking about blatant murder.

"Well, I won't do anything so horrible," I said. "It seems different here. I've seen so much death going back in history. But I'm the modern me, even if I'm living in the 17th century. So I won't become less of myself."

The tip of his tongue, hot and gentle, slid over my eyelids, both eyes and lashes. He said, "You, my precious one, are so much yourself that I cannot resist you and do not wish to. Sarah Harrington is also considering the rights and wrongs of killing her husband. Remember, she is also you. No one else inhabits you but yourself throughout the incarnations we suffer."

"So you kissed her – being me?"

"I wed Tilda, then found that what I loved in her had grown in you. You are more Tilda than she was and Sarah Harrington is a part of you, as Tilda was. But not all of you. So in only a few more essential moments I shall take you home to where we are simply ourselves, and where our son will soon be waking. Our grounds are cleansed, and what remains can be eliminated. Will you give me time, my beloved, for just those few brief tasks? And perhaps – just perhaps – one more?"

"You always know what has to be done." I couldn't judge anything my Vespasian told me, nor wanted to. All I wanted was my own home, my own beloved son, and to curl in my husband's arms. And also – of course – to wander my garden when the spring came, without treading on demonic toes.

"I shall instantly go to Cromwell and back here then, my love, to fly home faster than any plane." Vespasian pressed me back against the attic wall with the irregular daub behind my shoulders, and kissed me before leaving. I felt his breath like wine in my throat, but hot as if mulled and spiced. I almost swallowed his breath like a medicine, and then felt the even greater heat of his tongue as it tasted mine. When he released me, his arms remained around me as he gently kissed across my eyelids and then my forehead. When he released me fully, I wanted to grab hold of him, but didn't. I wasn't quite so silly, especially after four years of marriage. But here in the ugly days of the reformation, I had seen far too little of him.

I let him go, not that I could have stopped him doing anything he wanted, and sat staring at the sleeping lump on the next bed.

Fleetingly I entered Sarah's mind. She had opened the door into her husband's bedroom, and was gazing over at him as he lay in the shadows of his great posted mattress. She had a knife in her hand. It was a long one, the blade slightly curved. It was shining in the starlight through the one open shutter.

But she didn't approach the bed. Arthur was snoring lightly, turning a little with his mouth half covered by pillows. The knife hung loose in her hand and she knew she couldn't, shouldn't do it.

I knew how she felt, for I wouldn't do it either.

But she lurched, feeling a rush of nausea. Simply seeing the man lying there made her sick.

Her thoughts raced back through the horror, the cruelty, the injustice, misery, humiliation and pain. A thousand times thrown to the bed and treated as a slave. No - far worse than a slave. She had been treated as a lump of inanimate flesh. He had loved hurting her and had often spent the day imagining how he might hurt her more, inventing newly adventurous possibilities, all of which delighted him, until he imagined something even worse.

The air dithered, and I was tugged, gasping for breath, into both existences. I was myself, longing to leave, but staring at the woman who mistreated her nephew and who had raped numerous young boys before murdering with malice and torture, the man who was doing exactly the same that she did herself.

Then I was Sarah, staring into the shadows at the figure in the bed and reliving his years of foul and agonising abuse.

There was a sudden click. I didn't know who I was. I was her, and me, and she was me, and I was everybody and cold wet suffering splashed its bitter freeze across my eyes. Vespasian's kisses disappeared. Sarah and I shared the same terrifying headache, and our sight was blurred. I knew the knife I had brought for protection from the kitchens was now in my hand, and I held it tightly with the rough wooden handle grazing against my fingers, but I was also clutching the long hilt of the carving knife held by Sarah. The wooden hilt was solid and smooth, and the ridge that kept my hand from the blade was brass and bright. I felt both knives. Somehow my right hand grasped both knives loosely at my side.

Even quieter than a whisper, I began to whisper to myself. But I was Sarah. "The church tells us of Satan and the wickedness of his witches and demons. So many sad women have been hanged by the state, and yet I am sure most were innocent. But now I have seen the demon dragged from you, my husband. You've housed that thing for so many years. But you are worse than any witch. And the one man I have known who truly held magical power, has been the most wondrous and beloved human I have ever known. The church is wrong. Yet magic does exist."

Between us, my two selves, my sight and my brain were blurred, and I struggled to know what I should do. I was losing all comprehension when shadows formed, looming up before me. Two creatures, one imposed upon the other, an absurd and monstrous ugliness where four eyes were splattered across one face. But the fury was singular, the great double mouth opening as the roar was both deeply masculine and shrilly feminine at one instant, and then the same hands lunged.

Two hands – four hands – long nails and then short stumps – as one body reared – then another – and finally I felt one hand grab my hair while another clasped its fat fingers around my throat.

Arthur's yellowing teeth were in my face while Agnes reared up and grabbed at Sarah. Then we were indivisible. I felt Sarah's knife in my hand and could have killed Agnes while Sarah held my knife, threatening Arthur. Then it was my knife in my hand but it was Arthur's face leering at me. I could no longer know who I was. I was no one. Or I was everyone.

Falling – me falling – Sarah falling – and then the great weight of two bodies hurtling onto me.

Still dazed, I struggled to separate both of me and both of them. Agnes was awake and her eyes held more venom than I'd ever seen in her, even when describing the pleasure of murdering William. She lunged and her fingers clawed at my face while her other hand fisted my hair, tugging like a wild cat until I felt the roots surrender. She snarled but I could hardly hear her. "A man – in my room – the head of a demon – pain – witches – in my bed."

Yet at the same moment I was struggling with Arthur. His strength was greater, and his fury was greater. I was Sarah, and he was the man who had tortured me night after wretched night across the years. Now he accused me of torturing him and of witchcraft.

I had once known another Arthur. A man so vile and so evil, he had worshipped Lilith. Tilda had suffered so much at his hands, and Vespasian had killed him. Another Arthur, worshipping demons, and now Sarah had suffered at this Arthur's hands, and this time I was going to kill him. Or she was. But that was the same thing.

And being Sarah, I knew his teeth were long, and I'd felt his bite many times before, even tearing pieces from my flesh as though a cannibal.

"A witch," he roared. "I married a witch. I'll chain you to this bed, witch, and call Cromwell to have you burned for heresy. Heretics are burned alive, witch, and I'll stand and watch your skin blister and your flesh peel off your bones as you howl and plead."

I shouted back at him. So did Sarah because I was her too. She yelled at Arthur, and I yelled at Agnes and it was all the same thing. "Demon," we shouted. "I'm no witch. 'Tis you. I saw the demon pulled screeching from your head."

"I've long thought you a witch," Arthur clawed now at my eyes, "and if I had a demon in me, then t'was you as put it there. I'll have you whipped, then I'll have you roped to the stake and light the fire myself." His grin made both of me heave. "Imagine, witch, as the flames rise up to your groin. Your skin peels off. Your legs are exposed and the fire licks at the hair you keep curled below your belly. I'll dance while you scream."

At the same moment Agnes shrieked, "Demons, bitch – I felt my body wracked as you forced the demon inside me. I killed that bugger William because you crawled inside me as a witch and murderer, and I'll tell the church about it. I reckon they'll accuse you of murder and they'll hang your miserable body on the gibbet. And as you swing there, wriggling and screaming, I'll stand below and kick at your bare feet. I'll laugh when you breathe your last and the piss trickles down your legs. A witch you are, and a witch you'll die. I heard it all in my dreams."

Arthur was bellowing, now both his hands around my neck and squeezing tight. "The church knows all about demons and witches. They'll have you on trial before you can summon any more demons. Cromwell knows what should be done. Unless I kill you first."

I lost my breath and felt the force of Arthur's fingers around my throat. I was dizzy, felt myself falling, but they were Agnes's fingers, and I wasn't falling, at all I was stabbing out at her, panic in my stomach, and it was Agnes falling. She wore Arthur's face.

It was the moment when both Sarah and I grabbed our knives and thrust them up and out – two knives in the same direction – and then one knife and one hand. Two screams and then merging into one scream. The same blood on the same hands.

For a moment I was only me and I recognised the violence of my own impetus, and the squelch of the knife point into the body on top of me. Another scream. Agnes reared up, then plunged down across my legs. My fingers moved, though I would have sworn I'd taken no action nor any decision to act. For a second time my knife plunged in the fat rolling weight clamping me down. This time the blade sliced into her neck and stayed there. Streams of stinking blood gushed and covered me. I felt I was swimming in a lake of blood.

Then the screaming and the rolling stopped, the weight stiffened and stilled. But then it began again with a man's grip around my neck and pressing against my throat so that I couldn't yell, and as the fingers squeezed again, so once more I couldn't breathe. But my long carving knife had already punctured his side, the blood was oozing and although his thumbs seemed inside my flesh, once again my knife was in his. I pressed it deeper, twisting and then releasing.

His hands dropped from my throat, and his own throat rattled. The carving knife hung from his neck like a scarf from a peg. He wasn't shouting anymore.

Arthur's body collapsed backwards and away from me when I pushed. Strange gurgling sounds rushed out with the blood like a little water rat mewling as it swam the river.

I just watched, mesmerised. It hadn't even seemed to be me. Sarah felt that I had done it, and I felt she had killed Agnes. Yet both of us were the same person, and we knew it because there was only one of us sitting there with two very different, but very dead bodies sprawled before us.

Both Arthur and Agnes lay face up now, their throats slit and the ragged flesh still pumping blood and their fingers twitching in the final blink of life. Or not even life, perhaps. Simply the impulse of dead and dying nerves. No flicker of eyelids frightened me and no whisper of a curse.

Both of me heaved, half sick, and pulled back from the lumps of ripped and hated flesh. Both of me were shocked, astonished, very frightened, and even confused at what I had done. I had never meant to kill. But the reactions of these living monsters had forced me into the desperation of self-defence. Twice. And I still didn't really know who I was.

Now Sarah was crying. No regret, but horror at what she had done, even though it was something she had yearned to do for years. Also, the fear of what would now happen to her.

The other me didn't cry. I had not hated Agnes as poor Sarah had hated Arthur. But I realised now that my actions had been foreseen and for-ordained. I'd had no choice. Stumbling from the bed, I slipped quietly down the rickety stairs from attic to garden and stopped there in the freezing cold, wondering what I should do next. I held a bloody knife from our kitchens, and my clothes were washed in blood. My guilt would not be hard to prove.

I knew Sarah's fear. Not guilt, simply fear. She would be imprisoned as a murderer, and would hang. I knew the same. I wanted to comfort her but when I was in her head, I was simply her, frightened and crying. So I couldn't even comfort myself.

And then I saw Vespasian.

CHAPTER TWENTY-THREE

"Are you talking to Sarah too?"

"At this moment, no," Vespasian smiled at me. "But she will soon know what I have done."

I almost hurled myself into his arms, but then I hesitated, one step from his tall shadow under the night sky. "Are we going home? Can we fly back to Randle? Right now? – But then perhaps someone else will be blamed for the murder. They'll find Agnes and they'll look for me – but if I'm not here they may blame Henry or the maid or someone else. And Sarah, they'll hang her. That would be horrible. I'd feel it was my fault. She did it, but she's innocent too. Though we still have to leave, don't we? Or I'll be arrested and thrown into Newgate or something. Then I'd be hanged and I'd really hate that, even if I come alive back in our modern world again."

Perhaps I wasn't making a lot of sense.

"They will not find Agnes, nor will they find Arthur," Vespasian said, and reached out, his hands on my shoulders. That felt like immediate assurance, a warm wave of comfort, before he then crushed me into his embrace. His whisper tickled my ear.

"Such untidiness, to leave corpses abandoned back in our history. Both the bodies have been removed. I have sent them to a place far distant."

"No one else will be blamed? Not even Sarah? Everyone will know it must have been her. And the blood?"

"Every path forward demands one step before another."

"And time,' I acknowledged.

"Time is the relevant answer, and every pathway is fashioned from time," he said, and took my hand, gently moving me from his embrace. "I will show you, if you wish. Proof is always a little kinder than simply reassurance. Bring Sarah, for she also needs to understand."

And so I felt Sarah's consciousness as we travelled. There was no sensation of carrying any weight, but I knew we flew through time. I had done this before. Yet it was the first experience, of course, for Sarah. She wasn't frightened, she was exhilarated, and her trust was placed in Vespasian yet now she also knew my voice, and without needing to understand what she called magic, she felt utterly safe, and utterly protected. She could feel us although not touch either of us, but neither of us needed to do more than watch.

The sky, which had been star studded, clouded over into a violent purple sunset. It seemed unreal, but it quickly passed and faded into the darkness. We sensed perfumes wafting over, as if time smelled of some delicious nostalgia, and the passing of it was a delicious kindness. Meadow sweet and blossoming lilac swirled into my head as though I was travelling on flower petals.

The next sign of light was sudden, no fragile dawn, but a brilliant dazzle of heat and light. I felt scrubby wisps of grass, and a hillock of burning dryness beneath my feet. I squinted. The light so glaring and abrupt after the undiluted darkness had left me blind, but I blinked a hundred times and rubbed my eyes.

The horizon was as flat as a table, and the sun scorched ground was pure gold. Hillocks rose and fell, rippling in the breezes, like a golden lake. Drifting sand dunes. We were in a desert.

Sarah had never seen anything like this, and her experience of any unusual scenery was limited. I had seen more, but I'd never stood before in such an endless nothingness of stretching heat. The immensity made me feel very tiny and very unimportant. I knew Sarah shivered, not with cold but with the heat, and for both of us, our clothes made us sweat within minutes. But the savage onslaught of the sun was soon so dry, it made me gasp for water, but did not burn me as a humid heat would have. It was as if the sweat dried up. I was on a cooking fire.

I saw buzzards gliding overhead like pterodactyl dinosaurs. For a moment I wondered if Vespasian had taken both bodies and myself now back to the cretaceous. A tyrannosaurus would eat the ragged corpses.

I looked to Vespasian, who stood very still beside me. Then he smiled and pointed.

Across a short stretch of soft sand, splayed on a sandy rise, lay two nightmares, each more blood covered than the other. A strange grave, there in the desert, their blood caked black and their open mouths raw scarlet, their tongues baked liked shrivelled sausages.

Dead, each stabbed in the neck, each neck torn deep and wide by the blades which lay beside them. The knives, strewn across the ground, were bloody. No forensic scientist needed to test for DNA since it was clear that each one had caused the death of the other. There was now, after all, no one else. And the horrific knife wounds matched the knives each had carried.

The man, in his pin tucked nightshirt and the remains of a small blue bedcap, lay on his back, eyes closed and mouth open, legs wide and both hands grasping at his belly where another smaller stab wound had bled down to his groin. His neck was open to the gullet. The entire body, rolled fat across the tops of the arms and legs, was reeking with spilled blood. The short, bent legs peeped from his nightshirt, and his hands, fingers clenched, were also blood stained as though they had clutched at the wounds before his final breath.

The woman lay close. She wore her petticoat-shift, equally blood stained with parts of the old worn linen so stiff with hardened stains that it hid the filth which lay beneath.

Her neck was slashed across, less ragged perhaps, but even deeper. The windpipe had been cut and the severed veins splayed out like worms from a nest. Her eyes and mouth both gaped open, her eyes glazed and her mouth dry over rotten and missing teeth. A small knife wound had cut one leg, but only a trickle of blood remained, like an ant crawling down her calf. Her legs were thickly haired, and the long dark hairs on the other leg had matted with the blood, as if it had been painted, hiding the dirt beneath. Yet streaks still patterned her flesh, thick yellow, where the piss had leaked.

A bloated belly swelled beneath the blood stains, breasts flat on her chest and flopping sideways beneath her arms. Her bare feet were thick with mud and so were her fingers, but her hands now rested at peace across her bulging hips. The face seemed strangely peaceful, eyes open and watching the stars, but the man's face remained lined with anger and the lips, although hanging wide, were curled in fury.

No decay yet crept across the bodies, but the buzz of flies, smelling death, surrounded both. There would soon be maggots in both mouths and insects rummaging in the open neck wounds.

Inside my head, Sarah was gulping, disgusted. I was not. I

understood. And then, I turned. Immediately she also understood for this was not England and nor was it the 17th century.

She nodded in my head, and I nodded in hers. Vespasian said softly, "When this is over, there will be no sign of attack, blood or death. You, Sarah, will check for blood stains when you return home, and remove any glimpse of what has happened. His body will never be discovered. Even the ruined sheets have been destroyed and the knife is here, hidden forever."

At first there was silence, only the whisper of the wind. Then I heard the soft tramp of hooves over the sand.

Behind us rode a group of mounted knights, and across their silver armour was emblazoned the sign of the Knights Templar. Even their horses wore embroidered covers and the reins were soft dyed leather. One of these knights dismounted and strode over.

As an intrigued audience, we wore unusual clothes, none appropriate to the centuries of the Crusades, and I was still blood stained. The knight took little notice of Vespasian, however, and did not look at me at all. He knelt, examining the bodies.

Vespasian said, "We come to fight for the holy land but have travelled from far away, and as we moved up from the coast, we saw this couple fighting each other to the death. My wife tried to stop them but was splashed with blood for her pains." Lies again. My honest husband believed in the old idea that since the truth was so valuable a commodity, it should not be wasted on those who did not need it, nor shared with everybody.

The taller of the knights now dismounted and walked over the dust and scrub, looking not at us but at his companion. They all seemed to accept our foreign appearance since all tribes, races and warriors came here to prove themselves and their ardent belief in their church.

"I suppose they should be buried," I muttered. "Or left out for the wolves and the eagles."

Were there wolves back then? Were there even eagles in the holy land? I shuffled backwards and wondered if we might be thought assassins. But death was all around us, and even those soldiers fighting for the Papacy did not seem horrified by the sight of unknown and mutilated corpses.

The first knight who had knelt to see and touch the bodies, now stood and walked back to his waiting horse. "I see nothing familiar concerning either of these folk," he said, dismissing them. "They might be part of some local family, distracted by some domestic feud. They might not even be Christians. I'll not concern myself with them and have a mission far more important. Bury these poor souls if you wish."

He was astride now but the second knight stopped, one hand to his reigns, and looked at Vespasian. "Do I know you, sir? Something familiar calls at me from your eyes."

"I once lived in Granada under the rule of the Moors as they invented the system of irrigating the land. I have lived amongst the Turks and amongst the priests at the Papacy. I have lived long years in England, in France, Italy and in the island of Sicily. Once I joined an English force sent by the king and encouraged to join the battles of these crusades. You may know me indeed, sir, yet I do not remember any friendship."

He appeared disappointed, first hesitated, but then nodded, and mounted. I watched as the small troop was riding off, then said, "It's around a thousand years ago, isn't it! We've dumped our own misdeeds back in history." I almost laughed but you can't laugh with dead bodies you've killed yourself at your feet. "Do we bury them?"

"No," Vespasian said. "Leave them for the buzzards. To bury a man before he is born will not benefit him." And once again he took my hand.

"You knew that knight, didn't you?" I half asked, half accused.

"Yes," Vespasian said. although not smiling. "He was a fool

who caused the death of many. But what is passed is past, even though we stand here within it."

"And little Tom?" I remembered.

"He'll be taken into the care of your school's headmaster, Henry," Vespasian told me. "And Sarah Harrington will change her clothes, destroy those covered in her husband's blood and then announce to the staff that Lord Harrington has left on some mission he refused to explain to her. She will await his return, but his return will not come. After two years, he will be proclaimed dead, and she will inherit the property and money he has left. Shortly after this Cromwell will also be dead, Charles II will come to the throne, and life will slip into a new pattern of pleasurable wealth and sexual freedom. Indeed, amongst those wealthy enough to prosper whatever the situation, there was considerable sexual abandon. And while the new king generously entitled and enriched those women he took as mistresses, many of those who had fought for him, or whose husbands had died for him, died penniless."

I said, "Oh, how horrid, but also how glorious. Cromwell gone, and music, dancing and loving all returned and accepted as beautiful again." I thought I could feel Sarah smiling, hearing and knowing. Then I thought of something else. "And did they stop believing in witches and sorcerers? Did they stop persecuting the innocent?"

"No one is ever entirely innocent," Vespasian smiled, looking out to that incredible distant horizon of endless flat sand. "Including us, I confess. But yes, the persecution of those who had practised herbal remedies to help the sick, were no longer called wicked. Charles II was no fanatic and practised disinterest, which he called tolerance. Persecution, however, was still accepted as proper by many people. Puritan belief continued for many years. Many simple folk had been impregnated with those beliefs and could not so quickly deny them. Some remained fanatical, and loathing the new tolerance, shipped themselves off to the recently discovered continent of America where they might live as they wished. We have later called them the Pilgrim Fathers."

"So there were Puritans practising fanatical intolerance, while the new king danced off to his hundred whores and mistresses?"

"A little variety is always interesting," Vespasian said through his smile.

That huge blazing nothingness was glorious, and I couldn't stop breathing it in and staring out, fascinated. Now, even though death lay heavy at my feet, I could smell only the endless baking heat. But I said, "So let's fly back to the tolerance of modern disinterest, because I love the one and only sorcerer I know. And then he can take me to bed."

Vespasian laughed softly. "We shall. Randle will notice nothing different. Whereas you, my beloved, will be offered neither freedom nor inheritance, since I have no intention of leaving you at any time nor at all. Once we are home, I shall fulfil my cravings, wicked or otherwise."

"At last? Really home? Oh, my love, I am longing to get back home, and our own bed and Randle and even stirring the custard."

But now, very gradually the first drifting reek of death began to claw at me. Others smelled it too, and I gazed up as I saw the stark shadows black against the gold.

"The buzzards," Vespasian said, and for a moment I watched them land, their wings almost floating, their bright eyes round and wide, but on the sand, they hopped, nervous, eager to leap at the sweltering delight of the food lying, inviting them. They were wishing us far away.

I turned at once, ready to ask Vespasian for an immediate departure, but before I said a word, I was crushed into his arms, my face squeezed against him, and the heat, the desert and the stench drifted away on the breeze. He leaned forwards as the horror of those vile corpses faded into sudden moonlight and kissed me. I imagined I might still sense the vestiges of the open sands and the emptiness of scrubland and desert. But I could no longer smell death. Soon it was just the magical touch of Vespasian's hands in my hair and his lips on mine.

CHAPTER TWENTY-FOUR

L ying on the long cream couch, long enough for his legs stretched out and more, Vespasian seemed asleep with both arms around Randle, who also slept, cuddled against him. The book Randle had been supposedly reading was now on the floor, open at *Cinderella and the Magic Shoes* and Vespasian had been listening to Grieg's *Mountain King,* which was now fading into the distance as the kettle simmered in the kitchen. I made the tea and carried it back into the living room., carefully ignoring the long, uncurtained windows.

Vespasian looked asleep but was awake. I murmured, "Where are you darling? I need you. Don't wake Randle if you can help it."

"The rustle of time," Vespasian murmured back. His eyes remained shut but the smile proved he was awake. He mumbled as though half asleep, "Is it Christmas yet, my love?"

"You know perfectly well it isn't," I said. "It's the fifth of January, twelfth night. We ought to be taking down our decorations, and it's the tree outside I wanted you to look at again."

With Randle's somewhat eccentric help, Vespasian had decorated the huge spruce in our grounds, which sat just on the banks of the lake. It was not in our direct line of vision from decked veranda to water but stood forwards at one side. Between them, they had made it splendid, crowned in silver light, twining silver leaves around its entire height, tiny balls of silver glitter and the cascading threads of metallic silver ice.

And there, within the glorious silver sparks and sparkles, the trunk of the tree shivered with life. The thing which had nestled itself beneath the bark, like a huge lizard all dressed for the Christmas parade, was the same thing which had previously inhabited the old oak. The thing gleamed crimson through the dark trunk, spoiling our silver glory.

The decorations were reflected in the little lake, shimmering so beautifully each night. But the demon left no reflection.

Now, shivering in the early frost, I stood with Vespasian on the edge of the decking and pointed.

Our little forest was still a flashing mess of ugly vendetta and enmity with nine demonic beings clawing for attention. They straddled the trees and the calm waters of our lake. Some spoke, when they could, although some slept as if waiting for the right moment to awake and attack. Now, however, realising how Vespasian had destroyed the three greatest towers of hatred, the others hated us more, and being both fearsome and fearing, either hid, quivering, or glared out as they planned revenge

Pointing again, I said, "Can't we get it out of that tree? Randle loved it when you first put up the lights and the decorations."

"Twelfth night means the silver falls today. I shall do this later. But perhaps the destruction of the nine should begin," he was still smiling. "One by one, my love, I must admit. For although not any of these has the strength to fight me, nor even to protect itself against me, the power I need for only one entire destruction must first be nurtured. Those I destroyed in our travels were weaker by far, since we caught each during their earlier lives. But these remaining nine have absorbed so many within, each will be as if battling fifteen or more combined."

"Teach me properly then," I insisted. "I didn't tell you before because I felt rather stupid, but I tried to kill the Agnes demon before you came and did it yourself. I'd seen you. I knew what to do. I just couldn't do it."

He wrapped one arm around my waist, and I loved his warmth against my shivering back.

"The next time," he said softly, "I shall bring you into the early stages. As the Gatekeeper, you would have done this alone, perhaps more powerfully than anyone else. But you, my little one, in spite of your courage, are deliciously human. And for an inexperienced human, this would not be easy."

I leaned against his shoulder. "You said it won't be easy, even for you."

"None of these creatures can harm us individually," Vespasian said, speaking more loudly than usual. His words echoed across the water and amongst the trees. "And if they combine, which is unlikely since hatred, damnation and cruelty are never friends to each other, but if it can be done and so is done, then I know myself stronger. They cannot overcome me, my beloved. We are as safe as the mice in our foundations."

None of that sounded as reassuring as I would have liked.

I mumbled, "But it'll be summer one day. Randle needs to play and swim, and I want to play ball with him and chase him through the trees."

Indeed, Randle was already banging on the windowpanes inside, knowing he shouldn't leave the house without us. Immediately Vespasian led me back inside,

Randle scrambled back onto the couch, another book back on

his lap. In a low chant he began to read the words. "Jack and Jill went up the hill. Daddy, have we got a hill?"

"No, little one," Vespasian told him. "Our grounds are flat. Easier to explore."

"A hill would be nice, Daddy. I could roll down. I wouldn't fall like Jack, honest. I doesn't fall over no more. But them silly pink and green people out there, they falls down all the time."

"They will be leaving soon," Vespasian murmured, "very soon, and leave our garden free for you to run and roll."

Reassured, Randle returned to his book. Vespasian and I stood together, Vespasian a little behind me, but his arms around my breasts and his mouth to my ear. "Shall I kill them for you, my little one, one after the other? And you will help me as I teach you and share my power. You have the empty goblet. It overflowed as the Gatekeeper, and that capacity can be refilled. But to keep it filled might involve something you'd dislike. So shall we call on the powers above, my love? And then I shall swing you over my shoulder, my hands on your arse, and carry you to bed."

I blinked over my shoulder at Randle, but he was too absorbed in his rhymes, so I giggled slightly at Vespasian. He was in one of those delicious moods which I adored. But I was worried too.

"I have a husband who became a reluctant friend of Oliver Cromwell and then presented the Knights Templar with a couple of corpses in the middle of the desert. You can do anything my beloved. Me? I hated the Gatekeeper. I don't want to be her again. And I'm not sure what the empty goblet means either."

"What we could do," he said even more softly, "covers so many possibilities, my dearest, that I doubt I could remember all, or even half. But those I know might be what you'd call an adventure. Not becoming the Gatekeeper, since that was the work of your interesting mother. But regaining power is very possible."

I didn't want to think about my mother. But that made me remember that I wasn't just an ordinary suburban English woman and instead carried an ancestral inheritance which I couldn't hope to understand.

Frankly, I'd never wanted to understand it.

A flood of strange ideas ran so quickly through my head, it seemed suddenly as though I might spend my life in ancient Egypt or flying over the Tudor Court. I would bet all the millions I didn't have, that Henry VIII had half a dozen demons tucked inside that fat belly of his.

So," I ventured, trying to sort my common sense from my imagination, "what makes the better solution? Us having some sort of terrifying adventure, or you destroying these things in our garden one by one?'

"The decision, my adorable beloved," he said with exaggerated enthusiasm, "is entirely yours. No best or better exists in such situations, since we cannot know the future, only the past."

It was the constant use of the word 'past' that suddenly brought back the shivers. My mother. The Gatekeeper. Samhain. Vespasian as terrifying as I had ever imagined possible for anyone. Tilda. And then, abruptly, discovering the mutilated body on the side of the road. I'd never met the killer but still went to his funeral. And now I wondered why, since I don't believe in coincidence, this had all happened at my own toes. People often ask, "Why me?" Well – why not? Why anyone else? But now I was doing the same thing. Murder on my doorstep? A copse of demons in my garden? Because of Vespasian? Or because of me? Yet none of that could be answered now.

So I mumbled, "But I can't make decisions anymore." And that was true enough. "I'm so happy to let you decide everything. I've been gloriously happy for the past four years. I suppose I've melted into a sort of mummy-housewife because you're better at everything than I am."

"I cannot even make custard, my love."

I interrupted his laughter. "Alright then. I need exercise. So – decision time. Give it another – what? – a week? A month? And then we can fly off into the wild blue yonder."

It was if I'd said the magic words, and immediately he slid into a different depth of thinking. "A touch more than a week, perhaps," he said. "I shall need to study our pet demons and discover which of them can be reduced to past trivia, preferably several within the same time period. A major excursion for only one annihilation would seem inappropriate. That will take study, my love."

Randle was taking no notice of our conversation, which probably seemed indecipherable to him. Cuddled up on the corner of the couch, he now had a pile of books, four or five, collected from his own private book shelf. He was now studying each one. Looking up, he asked me, "Mummy. Who is Harry in a pot?"

I had to think about that one. Vespasian interrupted, "You are somewhat young for Harry Potter as yet, my dear. Be satisfied with the Mad Hatter."

"The pot boy has a wand, Daddy. I like that. And I don't think that hatter is mad anyway. He's nice. Like you."

Vespasian accepted the similarity and smiled, looking back at me. "Our Randle is growing."

I had missed him desperately last time. So I said, "Can it be a quicker adventure? I just hate leaving Randle for so long. I'd even planned on volunteering at that little private zoo on the other side of the village. They need help. You know, they have two sloths and one has just had a baby, but she didn't seem to notice and didn't feed it. I took Randle yesterday, and that baby sloth is delicious. It's too much work for the couple of keepers they have, because it needs so much feeding and looking after. I thought we could have it at home until it can look after itself."

"I have never seen one," said Vespasian somewhat vaguely. "Bring it home by all means. Whatever journeys we make, we shall be away only one minute of normal directional time."

I could just imagine my husband with a baby sloth hanging around his neck like a woolly scarf.

Actually, of course, he wasn't my husband at all. He had married Tilda a thousand years ago, and that seemed close enough for me. We couldn't marry now since he had no birth certificate, nor even proof of identity except that tall graceful body standing in front of my nose. Identity enough? He did have a driving licence, but we'd probably have to forge papers again one day. In the meantime, we bought, sold, banked and did pretty much everything in my name, which didn't bother him in the slightest.

"So you don't yet know where we might go?" I asked, without needing to wait for a reply. "Now that's fun. But I remember you saying it had to be after Lilith's destruction. After the year 1210? That leaves us plenty of exciting possibilities."

I still stood at the window and saw the sudden swirl of bare branches from the oak, followed by the shuffle of the foliage amongst the decorations on the spruce. A silver star dropped to the ground. It didn't matter since today was the day for packing it all away, but I didn't want demons packed in a box in our attic.

Vespasian had wandered over to the couch and sprawled there next to Randle. He looked up. "Everything is possible," he told me, "but none of it is essential. Look," and he waved one hand out into the further shadows where our garden disappeared into the winter clouds. "They cannot enter. They cannot touch any of us. They cannot hurt us. They cannot even disrupt our lives."

As far as I was concerned, they were already disrupting mine.

Looking out on any clear day of pale winter's sunshine, I could see the pale shapes within the trees, distorting the natural colours and the flare of the branches. I heard them whine in the night, and sometimes even saw eyes glaring at me through the bark. A few times I had heard words. Twice the trees themselves had moved. On other occasions I saw elongations like hands or feet poking from the tangle of roots. Once I heard the rattle of branches, sounding like the rattle of bones, so even when the wind was indeed the culprit, I suspected the things within.

But with Vespasian's arms around me I felt a safety which defied everything. And Randle, who sometimes saw what I wished he could not, was not afraid. I watched him laugh, and point, and call them *"Leafy blobs,"* or *"silly sparkles."* Life was back almost to normal, and I adored it. Our nearby village was old, mostly thatched, deliciously pretty, and centuries ago had been named Wetherwand. I felt as if it had been named for us.

I gazed over at my husband and son, who looked so very alike, with their black hair and deep dark eyes. So I nodded. I nearly said, *"Any one for custard?"* but stopped myself. Instead I said, "When you decide on the time period, let me know. I can look it up on the computer."

And Vespasian nodded, leaned backwards against the huge cushions, closed his eyes as Randle climbed back onto his lap, and I knew he had started thinking, falling into the dark mist which seemed to be where he lived half of the time, and during which he would discover where and when we should travel next.

THE END

Until the next instalment, if you have enjoyed time travel as much as I have, then why not give 'Future Tense' a try?

Mercy comes home to her empty London flat after another

miserable day at work, she finds she is being haunted by a pair of eyes.

Is she delusional or is time the delusion?

Falling for a time traveller comes with plenty of surprises and a good deal of danger.

For another mysterious read get Future Tense here.

ABOUT THE AUTHOR

My passion is for late English medieval history and this forms the background for my historical fiction. I also have a love of fantasy and the wild freedom of the imagination, with its haunting threads of sadness and the exploration of evil. Although all my books have romantic undertones, I would not class them purely as romances. We all wish to enjoy some romance in our lives, there is also a yearning for adventure, mystery, suspense, friendship and spontaneous experience. My books include all of this and more, but my greatest loves are the beauty of the written word, and the utter fascination of good characterisation. Bringing my characters to life is my principal aim.

For more information on this and other books, or to subscribe for updates, new releases and free downloads, please visit barbaragaskelldenvil.com

Printed in Great Britain
by Amazon